WENDELL BERRY

Also by Wendell Berry

WENDELL BERRY

Nathan Coulter

a novel

COUNTERPOINT

BERKELEY

This book is a work of fiction. Nothing is in it that has
not been imagined.

I wish to acknowledge my indebtedness to the Creative Writing
Center of Stanford University for a fellowship that allowed me a
year of free time to work on this book, and to the *Carolina Quarterly*,
which published earlier versions of two chapters.

Library of Congress Cataloging-in-Publication Data
Berry, Wendell, 1934-
Nathan Coulter : a novel / Wendell Berry
p. cm.
ISBN-13: 978-1-58243-409-4
ISBN-10: 1-58243-409-3
1. Port William (Ky. : Imaginary place)—Fiction.
2. Country life—Fiction. 3. Kentucky—Fiction. I. Title.
PS3552.E75N28 2008
813'.54—dc22   2007044433

Book design by David Bullen
Printed in the United States of America

Counterpoint
2560 Ninth Street, Suite 318
Berkeley, CA 94710
www.counterpointpress.com

11

For John

Nathan Coulter

1

Dark. The light went out the door when she pulled it to. And then everything came in close around me, the way it was in the daylight, only all close. Because in the dark I could remember and not see. The sun was first, going over the hill behind our barn. Then the river was covered with the shadows of the hills. Then the hills went behind their shadows, and just the house and the barn and the other buildings were left, standing black against the sky where it was still white in the west.

After supper it was only the inside of the house, lighted where we moved from the kitchen to the living room and upstairs to bed. Until the last of the light went out the door; and it was all there in the room, close enough to touch if I didn't reach out my hand. The dark broke them loose and let them in. The memory was closer than the sight of them. What was left outside was the way it had been before anybody had come there to see anything.

I lay awake listening to the wind blow. It was the beginning of the dream, I knew, even if I was still awake listening. The wind came hard against the back of the house and rattled the weatherboarding and whooped around the corners; and went on through the woods on the hillside, bending the trees and cracking the limbs together; and on with a lonely, hollow sound into the river bottoms; and on over the country, over the farms and roads and towns and cities. It seemed that I could hear the sounds the wind made in all the places it was, all at the same time.

I never knew when I began to dream the wind and quit listening to it. But after a while the bed rose off the floor and floated out of the house. It flew up high over the roof and sailed down again to the hillside above the river. The wind pulled at the bedclothes and I had to hold them around my neck to keep them from blowing away.

Standing at the edge of the woods was a lion, looking up at the house, with the valley and the river lying in the dark behind him. I could see every muscle in his body rolled up smooth under his hide. The wind blew through his mane. His eyes reminded me of Grandpa's, they were so fierce and blue.

While I watched he lifted his head and roared toward the house, his white teeth showing and his tongue curled under the sound. I knew then it wasn't the wind I'd heard, but the lion's voice, lonely and like a wind. The muscles in his belly hardened and heaved the voice out of his mouth; and he stood quiet while the sound went on and on over the country. I held the covers around my neck and watched him, and heard his voice go through the woods and into the valley and against the walls of the houses where the people were asleep.

Late in the night the bed floated into the house again. And it was quiet until the roosters began to crow in the dark where the voice of the lion had been. While the roosters crowed I dreamed of them, their voices crying in the barns and henhouses, close and far away under the dark. In my dream their combs were red, and their feathers black as coal. And while I slept they crowed the dark away.

❦

Sunlight came red into my sleep and I nearly woke until I turned over and slept again in the shadow of my face. Then the light brightened and hardened in the room and I couldn't sleep any longer. But I kept my eyes closed, remembering what I'd dreamed.

I heard Mother walk across the kitchen floor and shove the teakettle to the back of the stove. I listened to her clear away the dishes that she and Daddy had used for their breakfast and begin cooking breakfast for Brother and me. The sounds separated me from the night, and I let my eyes come open.

Brother was still asleep on the other side of the room. He'd thrown the sheet off and was lying on his back with one foot sticking over the edge of the bed. I watched his ribs fold and unfold over his breathing. The sun hit the mirror on top of the bureau and glanced off against the ceiling. Beside my bed my pants and shirt were piled on my shoes where I'd taken them off the night before. My clothes were hand-me-downs that Brother had outgrown and passed on to me. His clothes were newer, not so faded as mine.

I pushed the sheet back and sat up on the side of the bed. Out the window I could see Daddy harnessing the mules in the driveway of the barn. He took the gear off the pegs in front of their stalls and swung it over their backs and buckled it on. Then he led them out into the lot and shook out the checklines and snapped them to the bits. I was too far away to hear the sounds he made. One of the mules kicked at a fly and I waited for the harness to rattle, but there wasn't any sound. He backed the mules into their places on each side of the wagon tongue and hitched them up. I could hear the wheels joggle when he started out of the lot. Mother went to the back porch, letting the screen door slam, and called something to him. He stopped and answered her, and drove on through the gate.

Across the hollow that divided our place from Grandpa's I could see his house and the two barns white in the sun. The back door slammed over there and Grandma crossed the yard and emptied a pan of dishwater over the fence. Grandpa's hogs came up to see if she'd given them something to eat, and smelled around where she'd thrown the water.

Grandpa and Uncle Burley were walking out toward the top of the ridge to meet Daddy and the wagon. Uncle Burley's two coon hounds trotted along at his heels, sad-looking and quiet because they knew he was going to work and not hunting. Grandpa walked in front; he and Uncle Burley weren't talking to each other. They got to the top of the ridge and stopped. Uncle Burley turned his back to the wind and rolled a cigarette. When Daddy came up they climbed on the wagon and rode out of sight down the other side of the ridge.

Grandpa's farm had belonged to our people ever since there had been a farm in that place, or people to own a farm. Grandpa's father had left it to Grandpa and his other sons and daughters. But Grandpa had borrowed money and bought their shares. He had to have it whole hog or none, root hog or die, or he wouldn't have it at all. Uncle Burley said that was the reason Daddy had bought our farm instead of staying on Grandpa's. They were the sort of men who couldn't get along owning the same place.

Our farm was the old Ellis Place. Daddy had bought it before Brother and I were born, and we still owed money on it; but Daddy said it wouldn't be long before we'd have it all paid. If he lived we'd own every inch of it, and he said he planned to live. He said that when we finally did get the farm paid for we could tell everybody to go to hell. That was what he lived for, to own his farm without having to say please or thank you to a living soul.

Uncle Burley didn't own any land at all. He didn't own anything to speak of; just his dogs and a couple of guns. In a way he owned an old camp house at the river, but it was Uncle Burley's only because nobody else wanted it. He'd never let Grandpa or Daddy even talk to him about buying a farm. He said land was worse than a wife; it tied you down, and he didn't want to be in any place he couldn't leave. He never did go anyplace much, except fishing and hunting, and sometimes to town on Sat-urday. But he wanted to feel that he could leave if he took the notion.

I stood in the patch of sun in front of the window and began putting on my clothes. The day was already hot. Hens were cackling, and a few sparrows fluttered their wings in the dust in front of the barn. I watched our milk cows wade into the pond to drink. Over Grandpa's ridge I could see where the road came up from the river and went into Port William. At the top of the hill a gravel lane branched off to come back past Grandpa's gate to our place. On the other side of town the road went down into the bottoms again and followed the river on to the Ohio. I couldn't see the houses at town, but the white steeple of the church pointed up over the trees and I could make out the weather vane on top. On Sunday mornings we could hear the church bell ringing all the way to our house. And we heard it on Wednesday nights when it rang for prayer meeting.

Between the hills white fog covered the river and bottoms, and trailed off into the woods along the bluffs. Grandpa remembered when steam-boats were on the river, carrying tobacco and passengers and livestock down to the Ohio and on to Louisville. But now there were only a few towboats pushing bargeloads of sand. The hills on our side of the river were green, and on the other side they were blue. They got bluer farther away.

Uncle Burley said hills always looked blue when you were far away from them. That was a pretty color for hills; the little houses and barns and fields looked so neat and quiet tucked against them. It made you want to be close to them. But he said that when you got close they were like the hills you'd left, and when you looked back your own hills were blue and you wanted to go back again. He said he reckoned a man could wear himself out going back and forth.

Mother came to the foot of the stairs and called us to breakfast. I shook Brother awake and waited for him to dress, and then we went down to the kitchen.

✻

Our mother was sick, and in the afternoons when she'd washed the dinner dishes she had to lie down to rest. Daddy made Brother and me stay out of the house then so it would be quiet. When the weather was good we'd go to the field with Daddy or Uncle Burley, or go swimming, or just wander around looking for things to do. And even though we worried about our mother's sickness it was good to have the whole afternoon to ourselves without anybody to bother us.

We went down the hill and into the woods that grew along the hollow between our farm and Grandpa's. Just enough air was stirring to tilt the leaves without rustling them together, and except for our feet rattling dry leaves on the ground the woods was quiet. We climbed the fence and started on toward the dry streambed at the bottom of the hollow.

When we'd gone about ten feet on Grandpa's side of the fence we came to Aunt Mary's grave. The grave was a shallow trough in the hillside, filled with sticks and leaves. There was no stone to mark it.

Our Aunt Mary had been buried there a long time ago. It was the first thing anybody remembered about our family, and nobody could remember anything else for a good while after that; we didn't know how many years it had been since she died.

Aunt Mary was our great-great-grandfather's youngest daughter. His name was Jonas Thomasson Coulter. And about the time Aunt Mary was grown he got into an argument with a man named Jeff Ellis who was living on our place then. Jonas thought the line fence between their farms should be built on Jeff Ellis's side of the hollow, and Jeff Ellis thought it ought to go on Jonas's side. They squabbled over it for several years, and there was some shooting done by both sides before it was settled.

While they were in the worst of this fight Aunt Mary took scarlet fever and died. Jonas Thomasson Coulter went down to the hollow and dug a grave where he thought the fence ought to run, and he made the rest of the family bury her in it. His wife never would speak to him or even look at him after that; but it settled the argument over the fence.

Jeff Ellis was afraid of the dead, and he wouldn't come close to the grave. So they built the fence ten feet on his side of it. That made Jonas's farm ten feet wider than even he thought it should have been.

It didn't really matter much, because the land in that hollow was steep and ill-natured anyway, and nothing ever grew there but trees and buck bushes. But Uncle Burley said that wouldn't have bothered Jonas Thomas-son Coulter. What he wanted was to own land; it didn't matter a damn whether it was flat or straight up and down, or whether it would grow tobacco or buck bushes.

That was all we knew about Grandpa's grandfather — his name, and how he'd made certain that Grandpa's line would run where it did. We didn't know where he came from, or even where he was buried.

It wasn't long after they buried Aunt Mary there in the hollow until one of the Ellises saw her ghost. She walked back and forth across her grave on dark nights, carrying a dishpan in one hand and shaking a dish-rag with the other one, the way she'd always looked coming back to the house after she'd emptied the dirty water over the yard fence. From then on a lot of people saw her, our people and different ones of the Ellises. Grandpa said he saw her once when he was a boy. And I thought I'd seen her a time or two, but I wasn't sure enough to tell anybody but Brother.

Her ghost walked because she wanted to be buried in the graveyard with the rest of the dead people in our family. But nobody had ever taken the time to dig her up and bury her there. We never even put flowers on her grave.

The top of the grave was caved in where the dirt had fallen into the hollow places between her bones. I thought her bones had probably rotted too. It would have been hard to dig her up and take her anyplace.

We'd waited too long. A big hickory grew up beside the grave, and she was just some earth tangled in the roots. It was strange to think of Aunt Mary being a part of Grandpa's farm, or maybe a hickory tree.

We climbed out of the hollow and walked along the edge of the big woods on the river bluff, then crossed the point of the ridge and went down again until we came to the hollow where Grandpa's spring was. Old Oscar was standing in the shade of the oak trees below the spring.

Grandpa had raised and trained saddle horses once until he went broke at it. And old Oscar had been his stud. He was a dark chestnut with a narrow white blaze on his face. He'd been beautiful when he was young, and high-spirited. When they were breaking him he kicked Grandpa in the face and left a long, jagged scar across his cheek. But now he was gentle. He was twenty-five years old, and he stayed thin because his teeth were bad. Uncle Burley said he'd finally starve to death because he wouldn't have enough teeth to eat with. He was blind too, and his eyes were as white as milk. It was as if he'd turned his eyes back into his head to look at whatever it was he thought about.

Brother and I spoke to him and walked toward his head. He rattled his breath through his nose and trembled until we let him smell our hands and he recognized us. Brother caught him by a hank of his mane and led him over to the spring wall. I broke a switch off a tree and stripped the leaves; we climbed up on the wall and onto Oscar's back. We guided him with the switch; when we wanted him to go to the right we jiggled the switch against the left side of his face, and against the right side of his face when we wanted him to go to the left.

Daddy and Grandpa always said that Oscar would fall down someday and cripple us. But he hardly ever stumbled. Uncle Burley said Oscar knew his way around the farm as well as he knew the inside of his skin. He had it all in his head. He didn't need to see it. In a way, Oscar walked and grazed and drank in his own mind.

Brother guided him around the spring and along the side of the hill to the Coulter Branch hollow, and then turned down toward the river. Oscar didn't like walking in a strange place, but we spoke to him and encouraged him, and before long he got used to the slant of the hill. He walked slower, though, than he did when he was in the pasture, as if afraid the road might drop out from under him or a tree grow up in his way.

We followed the old wagon road down Coulter Branch to the bottom of the hill and turned upriver past the old Billy Hole landing where Beriah Easterly had his store. The river ran close to the road there. We took the path down through a woods of water maples and elms and sycamores to where Uncle Burley's fishing shack stood overlooking the river.

Once the shack had been painted green, but the paint had weathered to a color that was as much blue as green. The trees grew up close around it, and vines had grown over the walls and out along the eaves.

We got off old Oscar at the camp house and walked the rest of the way to the river. He stood still where we'd stopped him, as if he'd run against a wall and didn't know how to get around it.

We walked upstream along the top of the riverbank. Behind us the trees closed around the camp house and Oscar; and then we went into a patch of horseweeds and out of sight. The horseweeds grew high over our heads, and so thick we had to bend them out of our way.

"This is a jungle," Brother said. "Nobody ever was here before."

All we could see was horseweeds. We had to look straight up to see the sky. But we knew where we were, and we went on, turning the bend of the river.

Brother stopped and broke off two dead weed stalks and handed one of them to me. "Here's a gun," he said.

"We'll kill a lion," I told him.

Before long we crossed a gully filled with tin cans and bottles, and followed a path into the open place that Jig Pendleton had cleared on the bank above his shanty boat. From there we could look down into the bend and see Uncle Burley's camp. Oscar stood there with his head turned toward the river.

In the middle of the open place was a table where Jig cleaned his fish. Above the table an old set of grocery scales hung from a tree limb. A few worn-out nets were strewn around on the ground, and one of Jig's trotlines was stretched between two trees to dry.

The path went to the edge of the bank, and then stair-stepped to the water. We went down the steps and crossed the plank to the shanty boat.

Jig Pendleton lived there alone and fished for a living. He was crazy on religion, and when he wasn't busy fishing he'd fasten himself in the shanty and read the Bible from cover to cover over and over again. He worried all the time about the sins of the flesh, and believed that if he could purify himself the Lord would send down a chariot of fire and take him to Heaven. But he never could quite purify himself enough. Sooner or later he always gave it up and got on a drunk, and then he'd have to start all over again.

He'd invited Uncle Burley and Brother and me in to see him several times, and the inside of his shanty was a sight. He'd found an old Singer sewing machine, and thrown the sewing part of it away, and fastened the iron frame with the wheel and treadle to the floor. Then he'd wired a lot of spools to the walls and run strings between them, zigzagging and crisscrossing from one end of the shanty to the other. This contraption of strings and pulleys was hooked to the wheel and treadle. It worked like a charm, but Jig never had been able to decide what it was for. He just kept adding spools and string until it was more complicated than a spider web. The whole inside of his house was a machine that couldn't do anything but run. When he was drinking Jig would sit and treadle the machine and sing and shout and pray for the Lord to purify him. One night when he came home drunk he got tangled up in it and nearly choked to death before Gander Loyd came along and found him the next morning. Some of the missionary society women in town saved string and spools to give to him because they felt sorry for him. He had a wife and daughter living somewhere, but they hadn't had anything to do with him since he'd got so crazy.

A couple of times Jig had taken his boat out of the river and left the country. He stayed away a year both times, and nobody knew much about where he went or what he did. Once he told Uncle Burley that he just wandered around, looking at the mountains and rivers and oceans that the Lord had made. Since the Lord had gone to all the trouble of making them, he thought the least a man could do was go and look at them. He was as crazy as a June bug, but he was a good fisherman and didn't bother anybody, and he was Uncle Burley's friend.

Jig was busy loading bait and tackle into his rowboat, and we sat down to watch him.

"Hello, Jig," Brother said.

"Hello there, Tom and Nathan," Jig said. "How're you little children?"

"Fine," I said.

"We hunted for a lion up there in the horseweeds," Brother said, "but we couldn't find one."

"The lion and the lamb shall lie down together," Jig said, "and a little child shall lead them."

"You wouldn't lead the lion that lives in that horseweed patch," Brother said. "He'd bite your durned arm off."

"You oughtn't to cuss," Jig said. "It makes Jesus sad."

Brother was ashamed of himself then, and he hushed. Jig began to bail out the rowboat.

"What're you fixing to do?" I asked him.

"Fixing to run my lines," Jig said.

"We'll go with you," Brother said.

Jig shook his head. "No, honey. You might drown. It's awful easy to drown in this river."

"We can swim," Brother said. "We won't drown."

"Listen," Jig said. "If the Lord's planning for one of you all to drown, that's His business. But He don't want me to get messed up in it."

He untied the boat and began rowing up the river. Brother and I went back to the bank.

"Let's go swimming," Brother said.

He started upstream again toward the sandbar, and I went with him, feeling a little guilty as if Jig might tell the Lord on us. But when we got to the sandbar Brother began to take his clothes off, running to the water; and I ran too, trying to beat him.

I kicked my clothes off and ran out into the river, letting the weight of it against my legs trip me under. I felt the water slap over my head, and I swam down the slope of the rock bottom until the deep cold made my ears ache. I rolled over and looked up into the blackness. The current carried me along. I loosened myself in it, and held still in the movement of the water. I couldn't tell whether my head was up or down; I felt as if I could swim forever in any direction. My lungs tightened, wanting to breathe, and I kicked the bottom away from me and swam up until I saw a patch of light floating on the surface. I broke through it into the air again.

I shook the water out of my eyes and floated. The sky seemed a deeper blue after my eyes had been in the dark. Over my head a white cloud unraveled in the wind. The sky widened to the tops of the hills that circled around the valley. Inside the ring of hilltops trees grew along both banks of the river. They leaned toward me — willow and maple and sycamore.

I watched them, letting myself float in the slow current. I thought if I floated to the mouth of the river I'd always be at the center of a ring of trees and a ring of hills and a ring where the sky touched. I said, "I'm Nathan Coulter." It seemed strange.

Brother swam up behind me and threw water in my face. We raced back to the shallow water, and waded out onto the bar.

I found a flat rock and stretched out to let the sun dry me. It was warm and I felt clean and tired. Across the river a hawk held his wings to the wind and circled. The sky was empty except for the hawk and the cloud. I cupped my hands around my eyes. And then there were three of us — the hawk and the cloud and me.

❊

When we got back to Grandpa's place we turned old Oscar loose; he wandered off down the hill toward his shade trees at the spring. We went on to the top of the ridge and back toward our place where Grandpa and Daddy and Uncle Burley were digging postholes. The ground was shallow along that part of the fence row; they were digging to the rock and blasting the rest of the way down with dynamite. When we got there Uncle Burley was sitting at the edge of a hole, guiding the rock drill, and Daddy was driving it down with a sledge hammer. Grandpa was working at the post pile, facing the posts with an axe. We sat behind Uncle Burley and watched.

Daddy glanced at us between swings. "Have you all been riding that old horse again?" He had to interrupt himself to say "Ah" when the hammer came down. The sun was beaming hot, and he was sweating through his shirt.

"No," Brother said.

Daddy looked at Brother and then at me, and swung the hammer down. "If I see you on that horse one more time, I'm going to skin both of you. It looks like you can't hear when I tell you something."

Then he said, "Get out of the way, now, before you get hurt. You don't have any business up here."

He dropped the hammer and went to find the water jug. As soon as he was out of earshot Uncle Burley winked at us. "You'd better do what he tells you, boys. It's a bad day."

"What's he mad at us for?" Brother said. "We weren't bothering him."

"That's just his way, " Uncle Burley said. "He loves you boys."

Several sticks of dynamite and a coil of fuse and a box of caps were lying on the ground behind us. When Uncle Burley turned his head and began working the drill back and forth in the hole, Brother picked up a scrap of fuse and took a cap out of the box.

We went out the ridge again and took the road to town. A few patches of red clover were blooming along the sides of the road, and daisies and sweet clover. Big dusty-looking grasshoppers flew up ahead of us, their wings clicking, and dropped back into the weeds, and flew again when we caught up with them. Finally we moved out to the middle of the road to be rid of them.

The road went slanting over the top of our ridge past Big Ellis's pond and his house, then it made a sharp turn and ran straight on to where the town's ridge pointed off on the river bluff. Beriah Easterly's house set on the outside of the turn, and we stopped to see if his boy, Calvin, was at home. We knocked on the door, but nobody came. We guessed Mrs. Easterly and Calvin had gone down to the store with Beriah. Their old bird dog was asleep under the porch swing, but he just raised his head and looked at us and went to sleep again.

"It looks like somebody ought to be at home," Brother said.

I knocked again. We could hear a clock ticking somewhere inside the house, and that was all. Things had quit working right. Daddy wouldn't let us stay with him, and now Calvin was gone. All of a sudden it got lonesome. We went back to the road and didn't stop again until we got to town.

The town strung out along the road for maybe half a mile—a few houses and other buildings and the bank and the church. Except for the preacher and the banker and the storekeepers, about everybody who lived there worked on the farms. There was one side road but no houses were built on it. We went past the poolroom and on up the street to where the drugstore and grocery store and harness shop stood in a row along the sidewalk across from the church. The harness shop had been closed a long time. The harnessmaker died and the town didn't need another store, so it had been left empty. The door and windows had been boarded up and covered with political posters and cigarette advertisements, and Calvin Easterly said that bats lived inside. In the daytime the bats hung together like a curtain down the back wall. It was a scary place when we thought about it, especially at night. But it had been shut up for so long that we hardly noticed it was there.

Aside from the harness shop it was a pretty town. Most of the buildings were painted white, and tall locust and maple trees grew in the yards along the road.

Big Ellis and Gander Loyd and the Montgomery twins were squatting in front of the drugstore, leaning back into the shade of the wall. The Montgomerys didn't look at us when we came up, and we didn't speak to them. Grandpa had thrashed their father one time for calling Uncle Burley a drunkard, and none of them had ever got over it. They were always shamefaced and hangdog when even Brother and I were around, as if they expected one of us to walk over and kick them in the shins. Their names were Len and Lemuel, but everybody called them Mushmouth and Chicken Little. We walked past them to where Big Ellis and Gander were.

"How're you boys?" Big Ellis said.

"All right," I said. "How're you, Big Ellis?"

"Hot. Too hot to work. What're they doing over at your place?"

"Digging postholes."

"Whoo," Big Ellis said. "They're feeling the heat." He squinted his eyes and giggled.

We spoke to Gander and sat down. Gander turned his head and looked at us with his one eye. He was chewing on the end of a matchstick. "Hello," he said. He wiped the matchstick on the bib of his overalls and began picking his teeth. Gander never had much to say. He'd killed a man and lost an eye in the fight, and it always took me a while to get used to his one-sided face. He stayed quiet, even when he was in town, keeping what he knew to himself.

"Could you boys use a chocolate ice cream cone?" Big Ellis asked us.

"We had dinner a while ago," Brother said. "Thank you just the same."

"Aw hell, you can eat a chocolate ice cream cone anytime. Let's have one."

We got up and went into the drugstore.

"Three chocolate ice cream cones," Big Ellis said. The girl behind the counter scooped them up for us. Big Ellis gave her three nickels and we went out and sat down again.

"You boys ever get in a fight?" Big Ellis asked me.

"No," I said.

"If we ever did I'd win," Brother told him.

Big Ellis looked around at Gander and giggled. But Gander wasn't paying any attention. Big Ellis let it go, and ate his ice cream without talking anymore. He wasn't likely to stir any conversation out of Gander — or the Montgomerys, either, as long as we were there. It wasn't very good company. After we finished the ice cream we stayed a while to show Big Ellis that we appreciated his buying it for us, then we thanked him and left.

Up the street from the harness shop was the hotel. It was a long, two-story frame building with a porch running all the way across the front of it. Salesmen and travelers used to spend the night there, but now the rooms were rented out by the month, to old people mostly. Some of them were sitting in rocking chairs on the front porch when we went by. An old woman nodded her head to us. "Good afternoon, young gentlemen." She turned to the others and said, "Such fine young men."

An old man leaned toward her and said, "Whose boys are they?"

"Why, they're Dave Coulter's grandchildren."

"Well, God damn," he said. "Are they old Dave's boys?"

"Grandchildren," she said.

On a rise at the far end of town was the graveyard. In a way it was the prettiest part of the town — with its white headstones and green grass and flowers, shady under the gray-trunked cedars. From there you could see a long stretch of the river valley. Grandma said it was a restful place, and it was. But it was hard to forget all the dead people buried underneath it. In the summer it was easier to forget them than it was in the winter. In the winter you felt they must be cold.

We went through the gate and up the driveway. Toward the top of the rise, jutting up even taller than most of the cedars, was the Coulter family monument. It was made of granite — a square base, then a long shaft like a candle with an angel standing on top of it. Grandpa's mother had bought it from a traveling salesman when she was old and childish. Grandpa said she must have been crazy too. It had taken twenty mules to pull the base of it seven miles from the railroad station. And the old woman had been dead about five years before Grandpa was able to pay for it. On the front of the monument was written:

FATHER ——— *MOTHER*

George W. Coulter   *Parthenia B. Coulter*

1826–1889   *1835–1917*

Beneath this monument
the mortal remains
of George and Parthenia
parted by death
wait to be rejoined
in Glory

George and Parthenia were Grandpa's mother and father. On the other side of the monument was Grandpa's name:

THEIR SON
David Coulter
1860–

Grandpa was the only one of Parthenia's children left at home when she bought the monument, and she'd left the other names off — had forgotten about them, or was mad at them for leaving. But Grandpa wasn't flattered that she'd remembered him. The last thing he wanted was to have his name carved in four-inch letters on a tombstone. The monument had been enough trouble to him without that. He still got mad every time he thought about it. It was as if she'd expected him to write his other date up there and die right away to balance things.

It had finally bothered him so much that he'd sent Daddy to buy a new lot for the family. He said he'd be damned if anybody was going to tell him where to be buried. The new lot was way off on the far side of the graveyard. Nobody was buried there yet, and it was all grown up in weeds.

The angel on top of the monument had his wings spread as if he were about to fly down and write the rest of our names in the blank spaces. Parthenia B. Coulter had left plenty of room for whoever might come along. Uncle Burley said the angel probably would fly on Judgment Day. That kind of talk always disturbed Grandma; she thought it was sacrilegious. And so he'd usually mention it when the subject of graveyards came up. He said he could just see that old angel flying up out of the smoke and cinders and tearing out for Heaven like a chicken out of a hen-house fire.

A little past the graveyard gate was the Crandel Place. When we passed there Mrs. Crandel's grandson, who had come to visit her from Louisville, was sitting in the front yard playing with a pet crow. Old man Crandel had caught the crow for him before it was big enough to fly. The boy was cleaned up and dressed as if it were Sunday.

He walked over to the fence and looked at us. "Hi," he said.

We told him hello.

"What's your name?" he asked Brother.

"Puddin-tame," Brother said.

"Would you like to come over and play with me?" the boy asked. "I'll let you ride my bicycle if you will."

Brother and I climbed over the fence.

"Where's the bicycle?" Brother asked him.

"On the porch."

We followed him up to the porch. The bicycle was a new one. And he had a new air rifle too.

He brought the bicycle down the steps and rode it around in the yard. It was painted red and the sun shone on the spokes of the wheels. I wished Brother and I had one.

In a little while the boy got off and gave the bicycle to Brother. But Brother couldn't ride it, and it turned over with him. Then I got on it and it turned over with me. Mrs. Crandel came out on the porch and told the boy not to let us tear up his bicycle.

When she went back inside Brother said, "Let me try it one more time."

The boy said, "No, you can't. You might break it."

He caught the pet crow again and we went over to the corner of the yard and sat down under a locust tree.

"That's a mighty fine crow you've got there," Brother said. "Can I look at him?"

The boy said, "You can if you'll be careful not to hurt him. Grandfather's going to let me take him home with me."

"Sure. I won't bother him." Brother put the crow on his shoulder and smoothed its feathers. "Say," he said, "I'll bet you don't know much about crows."

"Not much. Grandfather says they'll eat about anything, and if you split their tongues they'll talk."

"I can show you a little trick about crows. You want to see it?"

"Yes," the boy said.

Brother motioned to me to come and help him. I held the crow while he got the dynamite cap and the piece of fuse out of his pocket. The boy came up and watched Brother put the fuse into the cap and crimp the cap against a rock.

"Here," Brother told me. "Hold his tail feathers up."

I held the tail feathers up and he poked the cap into the crow's bunghole. I gave him a match and he struck it on his shoe.

"Now you watch," Brother said. "You'll learn something about crows." He lit the fuse and pitched the crow up in the air.

The crow flew around over our heads for a minute, and Brother and I got out of the way. Then he looked around and saw that little ball of fire following him, spitting like a mad tomcat. He really got down to business then. He planned to fly right off and leave that fire. But it caught up with him over old man Crandel's barn. *BLAM!* And feathers and guts went every which way. Where the crow had been was a little piece of blue sky with a ring of smoke and black feathers around it.

Brother and I took off over the fence. When we looked back the boy was still standing there with his mouth open, staring up at the place where the crow had exploded. He started to cry. I felt sorry for him when I saw that, but there was nothing to do but run.

When we got back to the graveyard we were out of sight of the Crandels' house and we stopped running. The angel on top of the monument was looking in the direction of town. I could still hear the explosion going off.

Brother said, "He thought a lot of that crow."

"He was crying," I said.

It was late; but we wouldn't have supper until dark, after Daddy quit work, and we didn't hurry.

"Do you think Mrs. Crandel heard the explosion?" I asked.

"If she wasn't dead she did."

"If she didn't he'll tell her."

"Whoo," Brother said.

Big Ellis and Gander Loyd had gone home by the time we got to town. Mushmouth and Chicken Little Montgomery were sitting by themselves in front of the drugstore, and we walked down the other side of the street to keep them from seeing us. If one of them had pointed at us and said, "There go Tom and Nathan Coulter, and they just blew up a poor old boy's crow," we couldn't have said a word. The sun had gone down and the nighthawks were flying. I was glad Brother and I were together.

When we were outside town again Brother said, "We'll tell Uncle Burley about it when we get home. He'll get a kick out of it."

That made us feel a little better. But Uncle Burley was still at the fence row with Grandpa and Daddy when we got there. They were busy, and we didn't go where they were.

By the time we got home that evening Mrs. Crandel had telephoned our mother and told on us. Mother made us stay at the house until Daddy came in from work. We sat on the back porch and waited for him.

When he came Mother told him what we'd done, and he cut a switch and whipped us. He was already mad at us for riding old Oscar, and he whipped us for that too while he was at it.

"Now I know what that crow felt like, " I told Brother.

"That crow never felt it," Brother said. "He was dead before he heard the explosion."

The next morning Daddy said that if we didn't stay out of trouble he'd take up where he left off the night before. After he went out of the house Mother told us not to feel bad because he was mad at us. He was just tired, she said.

It started raining that afternoon, and rained off and on for a couple of days. The wet weather kept Daddy from working in the field; that gave him a chance to rest and he got into a better humor. He let us stay with him while he did odd jobs around the barn, and we enjoyed each other's company.

On the morning after the ground had dried Daddy hitched the team to the cultivator and drove to the tobacco patch. We watched him leave; and then we fed Mother's chickens for her because she wasn't feeling good.

After a while we saw Grandpa riding his saddle mare across the field toward our house, and we ran to open the lot gate for him.

"Where's your daddy?" he asked us.

"Plowing tobacco," Brother said.

He turned the mare around and rode back through the gate. Brother and I watched him go up the ridge. When he rode the mare he kept his walking cane hooked over his arm. Mother said he carried the cane because he was old, but mostly he used it as a riding whip. He could walk almost as fast as Daddy, poking the cane straight out in front of him as if to get the air and everything out of the way so he could move faster. He always hurried, even across a room, setting his feet down hard. You could never imagine him turning around and going the other way. When he walked through the house he made the dishes rattle in the kitchen cabinet, and you half expected to find his tracks sunk into the floor. He was tall and lean, his face crossed with wrinkles. His hair was white and it hung in his eyes most of the time when he wasn't wearing a hat, because he didn't use a comb for anything but to scratch his head. His nose crooked like a hawk's and his eyes were pale and blue.

Before long he came over the ridge again, and Daddy came with him. Daddy had unhitched the team and the wind blew the sound of the loose trace chains down into the lot. Grandpa rode through the gate ahead of him and unsaddled the mare and put her in a stall, and then helped unharness the mules.

"Did you get done, Daddy?" Brother said.

"No," Daddy said. He sounded mad again.

I was going to ask him why he'd quit, but Grandpa told me to get out of the way before one of the mules kicked my head off.

"They won't kick me," I said. "I feed them all the time."

He looked at me and snorted. "Shit," he said.

When they got the mules unhitched Daddy went to the house, and Grandpa led the mules to the barn to put them in their stalls. Brother and I followed him into the driveway. "Didn't I tell you to stay away from these mules?" he said. "Go to the house."

Daddy was in the kitchen talking to Mother when we came in.

"What's going on?" Brother asked.

Daddy didn't answer. He went out and started the car, and he and Grandpa drove off toward town.

In about half an hour they came back. Uncle Burley was slouched between them in the front seat. Grandpa got out and hooked his cane around Uncle Burley's arm and told him to come on out of there. Uncle Burley crawled out and stood up, holding on to his head with one hand and on to the car door with the other one. He hadn't shaved for two or three days, and his whiskers were matted with blood and dirt.

There was a knot on the left side of his head, starting above the ear and ending in a cut an inch long across his cheekbone.

"Hello, Uncle Burley," I said.

"Well now," he said, "good morning boys." He let go the door to wave to us and fell down in a pile.

"For God's sake, look at Uncle Burley," Brother said.

Daddy and Grandpa picked him up between them and helped him into the house. Mother filled a pan with hot water and got the iodine out of the medicine cabinet and followed them to the living room. They stretched Uncle Burley out on the sofa and Mother began washing the blood off his face. She was gentle with him, and washed carefully around the cut so it wouldn't hurt.

"What did he hit you with, Burley?" Daddy asked.

"Jack handle. Surely must have been a jack handle."

"It's a damned shame he didn't use the jack," Grandpa said.

Mother finished washing Uncle Burley's face, and then poured some iodine into the cut. He whooped and sat up.

Grandpa jobbed the cane into his ribs. "Lay down there, God damn it."

Uncle Burley lay down again and let Mother bandage his face. Then they got him up and led him out to the kitchen. Brother and I kept out of the way and watched them set him down at the table. Mother poured him a cup of coffee, and she and Daddy and Grandpa went out on the back porch and began talking.

Uncle Burley's hands shook so much that he splashed some of the coffee out into his saucer; he tried to drink it out of the saucer and shook it all over his shirt.

He saw Brother and me watching him and grinned at us. "Now boys," he said, "let Uncle Burley tell you something. Don't ever drink. It's bad for you." Then he said, "But if you ever do drink be sure to get to hell away from home to do it." He set the coffee cup down and touched the side of his head with his fingers. "If you ever drink, and you ever get in a fight, always try to make an honorable show." He laid his right hand on the table so we could see it. It was skinned up across the knuckles and the middle finger was out of joint. "Boys," he said, "I was after him just like a hay rake."

He finished the cup of coffee and Brother got the pot and poured him another one. He put an arm around each of us and said, "Don't let on to the rest of them, but Uncle Burley was drunk."

He told us to keep it to ourselves, because there were some things that were a man's own business. We said we'd be quiet about it.

"It don't pay to talk too much about your business," he said.

When he'd finished the second cup of coffee Grandpa and Daddy loaded him back into the car and started home with him. Mother told us to stay in the kitchen and help her, but she had to leave the room for something and we ducked out the back door.

We cut across the field and got to Grandpa's house just as they were helping Uncle Burley out of the car again. Grandma was in the kitchen cooking dinner. When she saw them coming across the back porch with Uncle Burley, she dropped a pot full of green beans on the floor, and stood there saying, "Oh Lord, oh Lord."

Then she hurried to help them bring Uncle Burley in. Grandpa told her to get out of the way; Uncle Burley wasn't dead yet, he said. Grandma's old yellow cat started rubbing against Grandpa's leg and purring. He took a cut at it with his cane, but missed.

"Scat, damn you."

The cat backed off a little, and then followed them into the house and up the stairs. Grandma fixed Uncle Burley's bed and they undressed him and put him under the covers. He really did look sick then. Under the whiskers his face was as white as the pillow. Grandma leaned over him and smoothed the covers and asked if there was anything he wanted.

"That's right, by God," Grandpa said. "You coddle him."

They looked at each other for a minute; and Grandpa turned around and started out of the room, the cat weaving in and out between his feet. He took another swing at it with his cane as he went out the door, but missed again.

Grandma looked at Uncle Burley and said, "Lord help us. I don't know what's going to become of us."

"Shhhh," Uncle Burley said. "It don't pay to talk too much."

She sat down beside him on the edge of the bed, rolling her hands into her apron. "Oh, Burley. Why do you have to be so bad, Burley?"

Daddy took Brother and me down the stairs.

"Is everything all right?" I asked him.

"It's going to be."

When we went out on the back porch Grandma's cat was hanging by a piece of string from a limb of the peach tree. It didn't look as if it ever had been alive. The wind swung it back and forth just a little.

"Look at that old cat," Brother said.

2

Our mother had been sick since I was born, Daddy told us. And she began to get worse. She had to spend more and more time in bed, until finally she didn't get up at all. Grandma came every day and cooked our meals for us and did the housework, and took care of Mother while Daddy was in the field.

Daddy got short-tempered with us, and stayed that way longer than he ever had before. He took us to the field with him every morning to keep us out of the house and we stayed with him all day. It was hard to have to be with him so much. Brother and I were careful not to aggravate him, but scarcely a day passed that we didn't get at least a tongue-lashing from him. He was worrying a lot and working hard, and the least thing could set him off. The worst times were when we came to the house at noon and at night. He wouldn't let us make a sound then.

I quit having the dream about the lion, and began dreaming things that woke me up in the middle of the night. I came awake sweating and afraid, but I could never remember what I'd dreamed. It always took a long time to get used to the room and the darkness again and go back to sleep.

On one of those nights when I woke up I heard Daddy talking on the telephone. I couldn't hear what he said, and I dozed off again until I heard a car come in the driveway and stop beside the house. The door of the car opened and slammed; and I heard Daddy's voice and then the doctor's on the front porch. They came inside and their footsteps went down the hall and into the room where Mother and Daddy slept. Before long the back door opened and I heard Grandma talking to Daddy in the kitchen. "I saw the light burning and thought I'd better come over," she said.

They went into the bedroom and it was quiet again for a while. I went back to sleep finally. But I woke again several times before morning, and each time I'd hear them talking quietly downstairs and tiptoeing over the floors. The last time I woke the sky was turning gray. I heard the doctor's car leaving.

Nobody called Brother and me to wake up, and we slept a little past the regular time. When we got dressed and went downstairs Daddy was standing in the living room looking out the window. He didn't speak to us, and we crossed the room and started down the hall to the kitchen. Grandma opened the bedroom door and came out, shutting it quickly behind her. Her face looked tired, and her eyes were red.

"Boys, your mother's dead," she told us.

She stood there watching us. I nodded my head, and Brother said, "Yes mam."

She walked down the hall. "Come with me. I'll fix your breakfast."

We followed her into the kitchen and sat down in our chairs at the table. The sun wasn't up far; the light came in at the windows and stretched halfway across the room before it touched the floor. Off in the distance I could hear somebody calling his cattle.

Grandma took the lids off the stove and kindled a fire. When it had caught she added wood and set the lids back in place. She put the skillet on and got out the bacon and eggs while the stove warmed and ticked in the quiet.

Daddy came into the kitchen while she was filling our plates.

"Here's some breakfast for you," Grandma told him. "Eat. You'll need it."

He didn't answer her. He went on out the back door. After a minute we heard his axe at the woodpile.

We weren't long eating. When we'd finished we went out where he was. He didn't notice us. We sat down on a log at the edge of the wood-pile and watched him. He took a chunk of sawed wood from the pile and propped it against the chopping block. He swung the axe over his head, sinking the blade, and drew it out and swung again. The chunk split clean, down the middle. Then he split each of the halves and threw them into another pile. Every time the axe came down he said "Ah!"— the keen sound of it ready to turn into crying, until the bite of the axe stopped it; and he tightened his mouth and swung again.

The undertaker came in his black hearse and took our mother's body away. Then some of the neighbors began coming. Big Ellis and his wife came, and the preacher and Gander Loyd and Beriah Easterly and his wife and Mrs. Crandel. As they came in they looked at Daddy working there at the woodpile, then stood on the back porch with the others and watched him, wondering when he'd quit and come to the house and allow them to speak to him.

Grandpa came, riding his mare into the lot, and stopped on the other side of the woodpile. He looked at Daddy for a minute, as if he wanted to tell him to quit or say something to comfort him. He looked away finally and sat still, only jerking the bridle reins a little when the mare got restless and began to paw and toss her head. Daddy never looked up from his work. The axe blade glinted in the sun and came down. Grandpa spoke to the mare and rode home again.

When Daddy had split all the wood, he stuck the axe into the block and started to the house. The people watched him cross the yard; when he came to the porch they turned away from him, embarrassed because they'd come to say they were sorry and the look of him didn't allow it.

They backed away from the door to let him through. He went into the bedroom and cleaned up. When he came into the living room he stood at the window again, not speaking to any of them.

The preacher told Brother and me that we should go upstairs and put on clean clothes. "You must be quiet," he said. "Your mother has gone up to Heaven."

"We know it," Brother said. "We knew it before you did."

As we were going up the stairs Mrs. Crandel came to the living room door and said, "Do you boys want me to help you get dressed?"

Brother said, "No mam."

"Do you know where to find everything?"

"Yes mam."

We went upstairs to our room and poured some water into the

washpan. The sun came through the window curtains and made their shadows on the floor. When the wind waved the curtains the shadows on the floor waved.

"Let's both wash at the same time," Brother said.

I said all right. We put the pan between us on the floor and began washing. Brother squeezed the soap and it flew out of his hands and splashed water on me. I splashed back at him; both of us laughed. He started snapping at me with the towel and I caught the end of it, trying to pull it away from him.

I heard a step behind me, and when I looked around there was Daddy. He grabbed me by the shoulders and held me clear off the floor and shook me. Then he put me down and caught Brother and shook him. He went out the door without saying a word to us.

I sat on the floor and kept from crying until I started to feel better.

"Did he hurt you?" Brother asked me.

"No," I said.

I got up and we put our dirty clothes back on; we slipped down the stairs and out of the house.

"If Mother was alive he wouldn't pick on us," I said.

"She wouldn't let him," Brother said.

I felt like crying again, and I could see that Brother was holding it back too. We started across the hollow toward Grandpa's place.

"I'm not going to stay here any longer," I said. "He doesn't have any right to treat us that way."

Brother kept quiet.

"Are you coming with me?"

"We'll both go," he said.

We heard one of the cars start at our house, and Big Ellis and his wife drove out the lane.

"We'll go and live with Big Ellis."

"All right," I said.

We found old Oscar at the spring and rode him out the gate and up the road toward Big Ellis's place.

"As long as we've got Oscar we're all right," Brother said. "If Big Ellis won't let us stay with him we can go as far as we need to."

"We can stay at Big Ellis's," I said. "He'll be glad to have us."

When we got to his house Big Ellis was sitting out on the front steps. He still had on his black suit; but he'd loosened his tie and taken his shoes off to rest his feet, and his shirttail had come out.

We rode through the gate and into the yard.

"We've come to live with you, Big Ellis," Brother said.

Big Ellis got up and tramped barefoot across the grass. He forgot old Oscar was blind and couldn't see him coming. "Hello, boys," he said.

When Oscar heard that, he snorted and shied and ran backwards into a flower bed. He hit a wagon wheel that Annie May Ellis had put there for a morning glory to climb on, and sat down on his haunches like a dog. Brother and I fell off.

"Whoa, boy," Big Ellis said.

Annie May ran out on the porch waving her hands in the air. If Oscar hadn't been blind he'd have run off then for sure. But he just sat there trying to figure out what had happened to him.

"Get that old horse and them boys out of my flowers," Annie May said.

Oscar got up and shook himself, and Big Ellis caught him by his forelock and quieted him. "Never mind about your flowers," he said. "Go on inside and be still." He led Oscar out of the flowers.

Annie May waited until she was certain that Oscar was going to behave himself, and then she did what he'd told her.

Big Ellis looked at us and giggled. "That old horse can't see any better going backwards than he can going forwards, can he?"

"He can't see either way," Brother said. "We thought we'd stay at your house for a while, Big Ellis, if you don't mind."

"What do you want to stay here for? We haven't got any more to eat than anybody else," Big Ellis said. He was still holding on to Oscar's forelock.

"Daddy's mad at us," I said.

"Aw hell, he ain't mad at you all."

"We'll work for you," Brother said.

"Well, I could use a couple of boys all right. But we'd better think about it first. Annie May's nearly got dinner ready, so you boys just as well come in and have a bite to eat while we think."

We heard a horse coming up the road, and Grandpa turned his mare into the driveway. He had a halter and a lead rope over his arm.

"Don't tell him about old Oscar falling down," I said.

"I won't," Big Ellis said.

Grandpa kept the mare in a stiff rack right up to the gate, then he slowed her down and walked her into the yard. I was afraid he was going to whip us, he came in such a hurry. But he only nodded to Big Ellis and told us that Grandma had our dinner ready.

Big Ellis took the halter and slipped it over Oscar's head and handed the lead rein to Grandpa. "I was about to feed them some dinner here," he said. He came around and helped Brother and me onto Oscar's back.

"I'm much obliged to you," Grandpa told him. He turned the mare and led us out of the yard. When we were going down the driveway he said, "Damn it, your daddy's told you to stay off of that old horse." After a minute he said, "And damn it, I've told you."

But he kept his face turned away from us, and he let us ride old Oscar home.

❧

For three days they kept our mother's body in a coffin in the living room. They kept the lid of the coffin open so people could look at her. They kept flowers around her coffin, and a lamp always burning at her head. The lights never went out in our house during those three days.

Grandma began staying with us even at night. She told Brother and me to stay in the yard or in the kitchen with her, and not to go in the room where our mother's body was. Once or twice we looked through the windows at the coffin and the people talking in the living room. But most of the time we stayed away. We'd see Daddy now and then walking around in the house or in the yard, but when he saw us he always turned around and went the other way. He'd changed and we didn't try to talk to him.

Everybody brought food to us when they came to sit by the coffin, until the kitchen was fairly stacked with cakes and pies and ham and fried chicken. Brother and I enjoyed looking at all the things they brought, but we didn't enjoy eating them. Mealtime always reminded us of Mother. It seemed strange to be sitting at the table eating while her dead body was there in the house with us.

Once while we were eating breakfast Brother looked at me and said, "Many's dead."

I said, "Minnie who?"

"Many people," he said.

We laughed. Grandma turned away from the stove and said, "Oh Lord, boys, you never will see her any more." And she cried, holding the dish towel against her face.

We cried too, and then she hugged us and told us not to grieve. She said our mother was in Heaven with all the angels, and she was happy there and never would have to suffer any more.

"Why, she's probably up there right now, singing with the blessed angels," Grandma said. She wiped her eyes on the towel and went back to the stove. "Oh, it's a pretty place up there, boys."

At night a few of the neighbors always came and sat up by the coffin. We could hear them talking and the chair rockers creaking for a long time before we went to sleep, and it seemed that we still heard them while we slept. We felt as if we never had lived in that house before.

For the first two days there were always cars parked in the yard, and people coming in and out. But on the morning of the funeral it got quiet. Big Ellis and Annie May and Uncle Burley had spent the night by the coffin, but they left early, and nobody else came. Grandma worked until noon, getting the house ready for the funeral, and then she warmed some leftovers for our dinner.

After we finished eating Brother and I went out on the back porch. Daddy and Grandma were sitting in the swing, talking. When we came out they hushed.

Grandma stood up and smiled at us. "Well, the boys can come and help me," she said. She leaned over and laid her hand on Daddy's arm. "It'll be time now before long." She went into the house and up the stairs.

Daddy sat there looking down at his hands, handling them, running the fingers of one hand across the palm and out over the fingers of the other one. His hands were heavy and big, with white scars on them that never sunburned. His hands never quit moving. Even when he went to sleep sometimes at night sitting in his rocking chair in the living room his hands stirred on the chair arms as if they could never find a place to rest.

Finally he looked up at us. "You'd better go help your grandma, boys."

We went upstairs and found her in our room. She had the bureau drawers open and was packing our clothes into a big pasteboard box.

"What're you doing that for?" Brother asked her.

"You'll have to come over and live with us for a while. Your Uncle Burley'll bring the wagon to get you."

We started helping her pack the clothes.

"How long are we going to live at your house?"

"Oh, a while."

"Why do we have to leave?" I asked.

"Your daddy's not going to be able to take care of you. He's going to be by himself now."

I saw that she was about to cry again. I didn't want her to do that, and so I laughed and said what a good time Brother and I'd have with Uncle Burley.

We packed all the clothes that were in the drawers, and then took our Sunday clothes off the hooks in the closet and folded them on top of the rest and closed the box. Grandma left to get ready for the funeral.

Brother and I went out in the back yard and waited for Uncle Burley. And before long he came, driving the team and wagon down the ridge toward our house, sitting dangle-legged on the edge of the hay frame.

He left the team standing in front of the barn and came on into the yard. "Hello, boys," he said.

It didn't come out the way it usually did when he said it. It had the same sound as everything that had been said to us for three days, as if it were embarrassing to be around people whose mother was dead. So all we said to him was hello.

Grandma came to the back door. "Burley, take Tom and Nathan in to see their mother before you go." She went back inside, and we didn't see her any more until that night.

Uncle Burley put his hands on our shoulders and went with us into the house and down the hall to the living room. When we went through the door I realized that Grandma had forgotten to make us dress up.

The people quit talking when they saw us. It made me uneasy to have them quiet and watching, and I looked down at the floor while we crossed the room to the coffin.

Big Ellis and Annie May were there ahead of us, and we stopped to wait for them to get out of the way.

"Ain't she the beautifullest corpse!" Annie May said. And she started crying.

Big Ellis looked around at us and grinned. "Howdy, boys," he said. His shirttail was half out, and he'd sweated until his collar had rolled up around his neck like a piece of rope. Seeing him made me feel better. I told him hello.

Annie May finished crying and we went up to the coffin. Our mother had on a blue dress, and her head made a little dent in the pillow. Her hands were folded together, and her eyes were closed. But she didn't look really comfortable. She looked the way people do when they pretend to be asleep and try too hard and give it away. I touched her face; it felt stiff and strange, like touching your own hand when it's asleep and can't feel.

The inside of the coffin looked snug and soft, but when they shut the lid it would be dark. When they shut the lid and carried her to the grave it would be like walking on a cloudy dark night when you can't see where you're going or what's in front of you. And after they put her in the ground and covered her up she'd turn with the world in the little dark box in the grave, and the days and nights would all be the same.

We went up to our room to get our clothes. The wind blew the window curtains out over the corner of the bureau where the empty drawers were, and I could see the barn out the window with the sun shining on it. It seemed awful to go. I felt like crying, but I held it down and it knotted hard in my throat. I took the pillow off my bed and crooked my arm around it.

"You'd better leave the pillow, boy," Uncle Burley said. "We've got plenty of them."

"It's mine, God damn it." I said it loud to get it over the knot.

Uncle Burley laughed. "Well, take it then, old pup."

Brother and I laughed too, and it wasn't so bad to leave then.

Uncle Burley picked up the box and we went down the stairs. As we walked out the back door they started singing in the living room. I listened to them, while we crossed the yard and went through the lot gate:

> *There's a land that is fairer than day,*
> *And by faith we can see it afar;*
> *For the Father waits over the way,*
> *To prepare us a dwelling place there.*

Uncle Burley set the box on the wagon and we climbed on and started out of the lot. I heard them singing again:

> *We shall sing on that beautiful shore*
> *The melodious songs of the blest,*
> *And our spirits shall sorrow no more,*
> *Not a sigh for the blessing of rest.*

My mother's soul was going up through the sky to be joyful with the angels in Heaven, so beautiful and far away that you couldn't think about it. And we were riding on a wagon behind Grandpa's team of black mules, going to live with Grandma and Grandpa and Uncle Burley, leaving the place where they were singing over her body. The sun was bright on the green grass up the ridge and glossy on the slick rumps of the mules. When we were driving away from the lot gate the people at the house were singing:

> *In the sweet by and by,*
> *We shall meet on that beautiful shore;*
> *In the sweet by and by,*
> *We shall meet on that beautiful shore.*

It was pretty; and sad to think of people always ending up so far from each other. We could hear Annie May Ellis's high, clear voice singing over all the rest of them.

"That Annie May's got a voice on her," Uncle Burley said.

He let the mules into a brisk trot, and we went up the ridge and around the head of the hollow where Aunt Mary was buried, and down the next ridge toward Grandpa's house.

❦

It was strange at first to wake up in the mornings and remember that I wasn't at home any more, and to see Daddy go away every night and leave us at Grandpa's. But before long we got used to the way things were and began to feel like a family again. Brother and I began calling Grandpa's house our home.

Things got pretty jolty there sometimes. Once in a while Grandpa would get mad at Brother and me and swat us with his cane, and then he and Grandma would get mad at each other because she always took up for us. The two of them didn't agree on much. Grandma said you didn't live with a man like Grandpa; you lived around him. And that was pretty much the way things were between them. Grandpa didn't feel at home in the house, and when he wasn't at work he spent most of his time at the barn. When he was in the house they lived around each other.

Both of them were usually aggravated at Uncle Burley. Grandpa thought Uncle Burley was a disgrace because he'd rather hunt or fish than work. Grandma didn't mind that so much, but she was always grieving because he was so sinful. He never was very sorry for his sins, and that got her worse than anything. But he hardly ever paid attention to their haggling. When they started on him he'd grin and ask them if they didn't think it was going to rain, and that usually put a stop to it. When it got to be more than he could stand, he'd leave and spend a few days in his camp house at the river. Brother and I stayed with him whenever we could, and when the three of us were together we had a good time.

We'd been living at Grandpa's for a little more than a year when Mrs. Crandel died. And the next day Kate Helen Branch had a baby. Uncle Burley said that was just the way things were. They put one in and pull another one out.

Mrs. Crandel's funeral was the day after that. Grandma tried to get Grandpa to go, but he wouldn't. He said the Crandels needed thinning out anyway. Uncle Burley and Brother and I laughed until Grandma made us shut up. After dinner was over and Grandpa had gone out she cautioned Brother and me about laughing at the sinful things Grandpa said. She told us it was an awful thing to speak that way of the dead, and that it was written down against Grandpa in the Great Book of the Judg-ment. Uncle Burley said he imagined Grandpa had been giving the bookkeeper about all he could handle for a good while now. Grandma told him to hush his mouth. She said that he and Grandpa were doing all they could to make sinners out of Brother and me.

"Tom and Nathan want to be good boys," she said, "so they can go up to Heaven where their mother is."

Brother was going to the funeral with her, and she'd said that I could go too. But I'd never liked Mrs. Crandel much, and I didn't like funerals, so I was going to stay at home with Uncle Burley.

While they got ready to go I went out on the front porch to talk to him. He was propped against one of the porch posts, whittling on a piece of yellow poplar two-by-four. The sun was shining straight down and hot beyond the shade of the porch roof. Down in the yard the locusts were singing. First one would start and then the rest would take it up, until it seemed they made the air and the sky rattle. When they stopped I could feel the quiet muffling down into my ears.

"Plague of Egypt," Uncle Burley said.

"What're you whittling?" I asked him.

"A piece of wood."

"What're you going to make out of it?"

"Be right quiet," he said.

I sat down beside him on the edge of the porch and watched.

He split off four chips as thin as a ruler and laid them in a neat pile between us. Then he started scraping them smooth, whistling "Molly Darling" through his teeth. He frowned as if he were taking pains to do everything just right.

Daddy came in the car to take Grandma and Brother to the funeral. Uncle Burley watched them leave, and went back to his whittling.

"When will they be back?" I asked.

He held one of the chips up to the sun and squinted at it with one eye. "Shhhh. Be awful quiet, boy."

He went on shaving and scraping at the pieces of wood. After he got them all shaved down fine enough to suit him, he split a thicker piece off the two-by-four and began trimming on it. The shavings curled all the way from one end of the piece to the other without breaking. He didn't let on that I was there at all. When he caught me looking at him he'd gaze off across the river and start whistling again. He shaved on that stick until it was round, then tapered the ends and cut four notches longways down the center of it.

"What's it going to be?" I asked.

Without looking at me he gathered up the pieces and lined them in a row on the porch. "Boy," he said, "I just can't think with you doing all that talking."

He got out his whetrock and walked down in the yard, sharpening his knife. There was a big maple by the fence and he walked around it a time or two and finally cut two forked branches. I waited on the porch while he trimmed them, afraid that if I bothered him again he wouldn't finish what he was making.

He came back and squatted down by the steps and started putting the pieces together. He stuck the little blades of wood into the notches he'd made in the round piece. Then he looked at me under the brim of his hat and grinned.

"Well, I'll be dogged," he said. "It turned out to be a water wheel."

We stuck the maple branches in the ground and laid the axle of the water wheel in the forks. Uncle Burley flipped one of the blades with his finger and twirled it around.

After he'd watched me twirl it for a minute he got up and started into the house. "Well, put it away now, Nathan. You can set it up at the spring tomorrow."

I took the water wheel upstairs and put it away. When I came down Uncle Burley was waiting for me in the living room. He'd put on a clean shirt and his newest pair of shoes.

"Are we going someplace?" I asked him.

"Well, since everybody else is gone, I figured we might as well go and see Kate Helen Branch's new baby. How'd that suit you?"

"All right."

"We'll just keep it to ourselves around your Grandma and the others. It's not any of their business where we go."

I said it wasn't. We went back to the kitchen and Uncle Burley got enough matches to last him the rest of the afternoon and stuck them in the band of his hat.

"It won't do to talk too much about your business," he said.

We took the road to Port William, and stopped at the grocery store. Uncle Burley bought a sack of Bull Durham and a box of snuff, and a candy bar for me. We went on through town toward the house where Kate Helen and her mother lived.

There were a lot of cars parked at the church, where Mrs. Crandel's funeral was being held; and when we went past the graveyard we saw the fresh dirt mounded beside her grave.

Uncle Burley pointed to the angel on top of the Coulter monument. "Chairman of the welcoming committee," he said.

"Uncle Burley," I said, "do you think Mrs. Crandel was good enough to get to Heaven?"

"Beats me. It's hard to tell what happens after they get them planted."

"Planted?" I said.

"Planted in the skull orchard."

That was odd to think about. It sounded as if people's bodies were like seeds and could grow up into trees after they were dead, and maybe those trees had skulls on them instead of apples or pears.

I thought how my mother was dead. But I didn't think of her growing up into a tree. Her body had to stay in the ground, but her soul was in Heaven because she'd been good. Grandma said she was happy up there with the angels. I thought it would be a bad thing to be dead anyway. I figured it was probably darker there than it was on Earth. And maybe she missed Brother and me.

I said, "Uncle Burley, there's not any way to find out how many times they've got your name in that book, is there?"

"I reckon not." Then he pointed his finger down the road. "Well, boy, if there's not the prettiest little walnut tree you ever saw."

I looked, and it was, sure enough.

When we got down to Kate Helen's house, old Mrs. Branch was sitting on the porch. The shadow of the roof had moved until it ran in a straight line down the middle of her face.

Uncle Burley tipped his hat to her and said, "Good evening, Mrs. Branch."

She squinted the eye that was in the sun and looked at us. "Howdy," she said. "Is that you, Burley?"

"Yes mam," Uncle Burley said. He asked her how her rheumatism was.

"Well, it's summer now and it's better. But before long it'll be winter again and the cold'll cripple me. I just live from one summer to the next one." She laughed as if she'd told a joke.

Uncle Burley laughed a little too, and said that she looked mighty spry to him. He took the box of snuff out of his pocket and handed it to her. "Thought you might be needing some."

She said it was good of Uncle Burley to be so thoughtful of an old woman.

"We thought we'd come over to see the baby," Uncle Burley said.

"Kate Helen's yonder in the bed," Mrs. Branch told him. "You all go right in."

Uncle Burley took his hat off when we went through the door and said, "Well, hello there, Kate Helen."

She smiled and held the baby up so we could look at it.

"Well, I'll be dogged," Uncle Burley said. "It's a boy, ain't it, Kate Helen?"

She said yes, it was a boy. Uncle Burley wanted to know what his name was, and she said it was Daniel.

"That's a fine name." Uncle Burley laid his hat on the foot of the bed. Kate Helen let him hold the baby and he sat down with it in a rocking chair.

"Well, I'll declare," he said. "If that's not a fine-looking baby."

The baby stuck one of its fists up in the air and started crying. But Uncle Burley rocked it a little and whistled to it, and it settled down and went back to sleep.

Uncle Burley looked at Kate Helen and looked at the baby again and said, "Well, I'll be switched."

He motioned for me to come and look too. And I did.

"Now ain't that a pretty baby, Nathan?"

It didn't look like much to me. But I could tell that Uncle Burley thought a lot of it, so I said it was the prettiest baby I ever did see.

"Little Daniel," Uncle Burley said.

I went across the room and sat down in a chair by the window. And then Uncle Burley began telling Kate Helen how we were getting along with our work. He told her how most of the tobacco crop had ripened early, and how we'd already cut all of it that was ripe. He said we were planning to cut the rest of it in about a week. And then he talked about how many young squirrels he'd seen that year, and promised to bring Kate Helen and her mother a couple of fat ones as soon as he got time to do a little hunting. After that he said he looked for an early frost, because the katydids had been singing for about three weeks already. Kate Helen took a little nap while he was talking.

After a while she woke up and said it was time for the baby to eat. I looked out the window while she fed him, and Uncle Burley got busy and rolled a cigarette.

The baby finished its supper and went to sleep again. It was late and we got up to leave. Mrs. Branch came hobbling in from the porch and asked us to have supper with them.

Uncle Burley said we'd like to, but we had to get on home and fire up the coke stoves in our tobacco barn. He told her that the tobacco had a lot of sap in it that year, and we had to keep the fires under it so it wouldn't rot in the barn.

He leaned over the bed to look at the baby again. It was smiling in its sleep. "Look at him. He's seeing the angels," Uncle Burley said. "Well, I'll swear." He put his hat on and started backing toward the door. "Well now, Kate Helen, don't take no wooden nickels."

We walked home and went to the tobacco barn to fire up the coke stoves. Uncle Burley shook the ashes out, and then we took a bucket apiece and started carrying fresh coke to the fires. There was enough trash in the coke to make the stoves smoke a little at first, and it made my eyes smart. It was already dark in the barn, and the row of stoves glowed red-hot down the driveway. I could see Uncle Burley's legs passing back and forth in front of them under the smoke. I imagined that Hell looked like that. It was hot enough too when I leaned over the stoves to empty my bucket. My eyes watered when I looked at the blue flames crawling over the coals. It would be a bad place to stay forever, I thought.

When we came out of the barn it was dark, except for a thin red cloud stretched along the edge of the sky. A cool breeze was blowing and it was fine to be outside again. I thought it would be better to sprout into a tree than to stay down there in the fire.

"Uncle Burley," I said, "it's a bad thing to be dead, ain't it?"

He lit a cigarette and flipped the match out. "Well, this world and one more and then the fireworks."

3

For a week before the Fourth of July, Brother and I worked at Big Ellis's place, cleaning out a fence row. The fence was a good half a mile long, running all the way down one side of the farm, and we contracted to clean it out for five dollars apiece so we'd have plenty of spending money for the Fourth. We worked from daylight to dark every day except Sun-day, axing out the sassafras and locust and thorn and scything down the briars, with the sun as hot as it could get at that time of year.

Early on the morning of the Fourth, Grandpa hitched his team to the mowing machine and went to help Daddy mow a field of hay. After he'd gone the day began to feel like a Sunday because we weren't going to work and it was so quiet around the house. The sun wasn't up far, but already you could hear the heat ticking down like a flock of sparrows on the back porch roof.

In a little while Uncle Burley came out and asked Brother and me to help him with a little work before we left for the Fourth of July picnic. We followed him to the smokehouse. He went inside and came out with a long-handled dip net.

"What're you going to do?" I asked him.

"It would be bad for a man to pass up a chance to make some money, wouldn't it?"

"I suppose it would," I said.

He sent me to the corncrib to get an ear of corn, and when I came back we went down to the pond. Grandma's ducks were swimming single file close to the bank, dabbling their bills into the water. Uncle Burley shelled the corn and scattered it along the bank. When the ducks came to eat he dipped up five of them in the dip net. We tied their bills shut with pieces of fishing line to keep Grandma from hearing them quack and carried them to the barn. We found an old wire chicken coop and loaded it on the wagon and put the ducks in it. Then we got the long galvanized tank that Grandpa kept shelled corn in, and loaded it on the wagon with the coop.

Uncle Burley sat down and looked at the tank. "Well, all we need now is water." After a minute or so he said, "Well, we can fix that."

He got up and brought two buckets from the barn and pitched them into the tank. And we loaded two water barrels.

"What're you going to do with all this?" Brother asked.

"Did you ever hear why they call a duck a duck?"

Brother looked at me and laughed, and we gave up asking him questions. We harnessed a team of mules and hitched them to the wagon, and went back to the house to wash and put on clean clothes.

When we were leaving the house Uncle Burley swiped three of Grandma's embroidery hoops and stuck them into the crown of his hat. On the road to town he whistled to himself, letting the mules trot on the downgrades. Once or twice he winked at Brother and me and said, "A duck is a duck." That always seemed to please him, and he'd grin and start whistling again.

Before we'd gone halfway to the picnic we caught up with a man who was walking in the same direction we were going. Uncle Burley stopped and asked him if he wanted a ride.

"God bless you, brother," the man said. And he climbed on the wagon.

"Where you going?" Uncle Burley asked him.

"Wherever the Lord's fixing to send me."

"You a preacher?"

"I am, brother."

He looked as if he'd been a long time going wherever the Lord was sending him.

"I am one of them it has pleased the Lord to send to the four corners of the world to preach the gospel," he said.

He began to talk about unbelievers and the sin of the world, and who was going to Hell and who wasn't. The Lord had appointed him to be a witness, he said, to all the people he met. Uncle Burley whistled and spoke to the team, trying not to pay any attention. But I could see that he was getting aggravated. After a while he handed the reins to Brother and rolled a cigarette.

"A cigarette is as much of an abomination in the sight of the Lord as a bottle of whiskey," the preacher said.

Uncle Burley lit the cigarette and smoked, looking straight down the road.

The preacher said, "If the Lord had wanted you to smoke He'd have give you a smokestack, brother."

Uncle Burley took the reins again and stopped the team. He looked at the preacher. "If He'd wanted you to ride, you'd have wheels," he said. "Now you get off."

The preacher got off and stood in the ditch looking up at us. He raised his hand and said, " 'Blessed are ye, when men shall revile you, and persecute you.' Matthew, five-eleven."

We drove off and left him standing there preaching in the ditch.

"If he's going to Heaven I want him to have to walk every foot of the way," Uncle Burley said.

A couple of miles from Hargrave, we turned out the side road toward the picnic ground. Just before we got there we went by a pond, and Uncle Burley pulled the wagon off the road. We took the buckets and made a line between the pond and the wagon and filled the barrels with water. Then we drove on into the grounds.

The picnic ground was a fifty-acre field, and when we drove through the gate we could see automobiles parked everywhere, looking hot and shiny with the sun baking down on them. In the center of the field was a grove of tall oaks; people stood under them talking and laughing. Here and there a woman sat by herself in the shade beside a dinner basket. A carnival was set up outside the grove, the tents of the side shows in a double line, facing each other across a kind of street like the houses of a town. At one end of the carnival was a Ferris wheel, and at the other end was the dance hall where the Odd Fellows held a dance on the night of the Fourth.

Uncle Burley drove around the carnival and pulled in by the dance hall on the far end of the rows of tents. We unloaded the tank and set it on the ground with the long side parallel to the street of the carnival, about twenty-five feet from the tent next to us. That tent was a shooting gallery, and we could hear the rifles cracking and a bell ringing when somebody hit a bull's-eye. When we got the tank leveled to suit Uncle Burley we filled it with water from the barrels. We found five good-sized rocks and tied pieces of fishing line to them, and then used them to anchor the ducks in the tank of water. Uncle Burley scratched a line in the dirt in front of the tank and looped the embroidery hoops over his hand.

Brother and I drove the wagon out of the way and hitched the mules to a tree. When we came back Uncle Burley was walking up and down in front of the tank, twirling the hoops around his finger. Before long a big pimply-faced boy came over from the shooting gallery and looked at the ducks. He was wearing a little hat that he'd won at one of the carnival booths, with a red felt ribbon that said I'M HOT STUFF pinned to the top of it.

Uncle Burley twirled the hoops. "Boy, do you think you can ring one of them ducks?"

"Hell yes," the boy said. "How much?"

"Three rings for a dime."

The boy looked at the ducks and then at the hoops in Uncle Burley's hand. "What do I get if I ring one?"

"Five dollars cash money, plus the satisfaction of it."

The boy handed Uncle Burley a dime and took the hoops. He aimed a long time before he made a throw, and I was afraid he was going to win on the first try. But when the duck saw the hoop coming she stuck her head under the water. He made three tries and every time the duck ducked her head.

"Takes a lot of skill," Uncle Burley said.

"Hell," the boy said. He paid another dime and tried it again. He spent seventy cents standing there throwing those embroidery hoops at the ducks, throwing at whichever duck wasn't looking at him. But they always ducked in time. The boy gave up finally and went away.

"That's why they call a duck a duck," Uncle Burley told us.

A fat man in a wrinkled brown suit, who'd been watching the boy, staggered up to Uncle Burley. "Give me a try on them ducks."

Uncle Burley looked him up and down and shook his head. "Fellow, don't you reckon you're too drunk to throw straight?"

The man pointed his finger at Uncle Burley. "You're a liar if you say I'm drunk. I can ring one of them ducks left-handed."

"I'm willing to bet you can't ring one right-handed," Uncle Burley said.

The man took two dollars out of his pocket and laid them on the ground.

Uncle Burley laid two more on top of them. "Three rings for a dime," he said.

The man had the same luck the boy had, only he spent a dollar. After the first ten throws he got mad and started throwing hard, trying to kill the ducks. He never even hit the tank after that. The more he missed the harder he threw, and the harder he threw the more he missed.

Finally he turned around and hollered, "I quit!"

Uncle Burley picked up the money and put it in his pocket. The man watched him, swelling up and getting red in the face.

Then he shook his fist at Uncle Burley and hollered, "I'm a mean son of a bitch!"

Uncle Burley caught him by the necktie and tightened the knot until you could see the veins pumping in his neck. He said, "You don't look so mean to me, son of a bitch."

The man walked off, loosening his tie and cursing to himself, down the tent rows.

Pretty soon Uncle Burley had as many customers as he could handle. A crowd was gathering and some of the men knew him. They laughed and asked him when he went into the carnival business. He grinned and kept quiet, taking their dimes and gathering the hoops after they finished throwing. One or another of the ducks was always looking over the back of the tank, and that gave them something to try for.

Brother and I stood around and watched until it got tiresome. Nobody ever managed to ring a duck. After the first dozen or so customers had tried and failed, we went to see the carnival.

One of the side show tents had a sign on it that said THE WONDERS OF THE WORLD in red and gold letters. An old woman stood out in front with a loudspeaker, telling what they had inside.

"See the two-headed baby," she said. "See the big jungle rat. It ain't like the rats you got around here — ain't got no tail — all spotted and striped like a tiger."

Another show had a fire-eating cannibal and a woman who weighed eight hundred pounds and a turtle with two tails. We didn't go into either tent. It was bad enough to know such things as eight-hundred-pound women and two-headed babies could be in the world without paying a quarter for it.

In the middle of the carnival was a tent with pictures of half-naked women on the front, and a sign that said BUBBLES: BEWITCHING ENCHANTRESS OF THE FAR EAST. A crowd of men and boys had gathered around a ticket stand where a big-nosed man in a derby hat was making a speech.

"Starting right now with one of them old bloodboilers," he said. "Hottest — fastest — meanest little burlesque show you ever saw. The show starts in ten seconds, gentlemen. Only a few seats left."

He stood there a minute, looking over the crowd, then started again. "Gentlemen, it's as hot as a billy goat in a pepper patch. It shakes — it bumps — it bounces like a Model T Ford on plowed ground. Only fifty cents to see Bubbles unveil the secrets of the East. Gentlemen, if you suffer from heart trouble, high blood pressure or dizzy spells I beg you not to come in here. You won't be able to stand it."

He wound up again and told how Bubbles was the Crown Princess of Mesopotamia, and had been kidnapped and carried on a camel through the enchanted deserts of the Far East, and how she had spent six years in the harem of the Sheik of Araby.

While he was in the middle of this somebody piped up in the crowd and asked him if she'd take it all off.

He said, "Gentlemen, you will see Bubbles as fully clothed as she came into this world. That is, you will see her in the garment which the good Lord give her — her naked hide. Come in, gentlemen. We only got a few seats left. It'll cost you only fifty cents, one half of one dollar, to see what you can't afford to miss for any price."

A few of the men crowded up to buy tickets.

"Let's go in," Brother said. He looked at me and grinned. "Come on."

I wanted to ride the Ferris wheel, but I let him go in front and we got into the line at the ticket stand. When we bought our tickets the man said, "Now here are two young men seeking to further their education. Go right in, gentlemen. You'll never be the same again." That got him a big laugh from the crowd. I felt silly then with everybody looking at us and laughing, but we'd already paid our money and there was nothing to do but keep going.

It was so dark inside the tent after we'd been out in the sun that we could hardly see. But our eyes got used to it, and we stood around waiting for the show to start. There weren't any seats. About a third of the tent was roped off to give Bubbles room to put on her show. In a corner of the roped off part was a kind of booth made of old carpets, and beneath the front flap we could see a woman's bare feet with red polish on the toenails.

We waited a good while, hearing the man making his speech again in front of the tent, and now and then another bunch of men and boys came in. The tent filled up. Mushmouth and Chicken Little Montgomery came in with one of the last bunches, but they were the only ones we knew. I'd seen most of the others before, but I didn't know their names.

Mushmouth and Chicken Little were ashamed to be seen in such a place. While we waited they stood together on the edge of the crowd, pretending they were the only ones there. They were both a little drunk, and when somebody happened to look at them they'd grin and back up.

Finally the man in the derby hat quit talking and followed the last bunch through the door. Everybody crowded up to the rope, thinking the show was about to start. But he went into the booth where Bubbles was and came out with a little table and a deck of cards. He set the table up on our side of the rope.

"Gentlemen," he said, "we still have a few minutes before show time." He shuffled the cards and made them rattle down in a pile on the table. "There's nothing to ease the body, clear the mind, and settle the soul like a friendly card game." He shuffled the cards again, but that time he made a mislick and they fell out of his hands. "Excuse me, gentlemen. I've had a little too much of your good Kentucky whiskey, I'm afraid." He picked up the cards and shuffled them again, then thumbed three cards off the top of the deck and held them up. "I have here the queen of spades, the nine of diamonds and the four of clubs." He laid the three cards face down on the table and switched them around.

Then he looked at Mushmouth and Chicken Little, who were standing on the other side of the table. "Now, can one of you gentlemen pick the queen?"

The queen card had a bent corner and it was easy to pick out. Chicken Little looked around the tent and grinned, then he turned the card. It was the queen.

"You have a fine eye, sir," the man in the derby hat said. "A wonderful eye."

He turned the card over and began switching them again. "And now for a dollar, sir, can you tell me the queen?"

Chicken Little laid a dollar on the table and turned the card with the bent corner. He had it right again, and the man in the derby hat paid off. It seemed he'd had too much whiskey to keep straight on what he was doing.

Mushmouth and two or three others laid down dollar bills and the man lost again. On the next round about a dozen of the men laid down dollar bills, and Brother and I laid down a dollar apiece. He asked which was the queen. Somebody turned the card with the bent corner, but it was the nine of diamonds. The next time it was the nine of diamonds. And the next time it was the four of clubs. Before we realized what had happened the man had crossed the rope and was in the booth. Everybody was awfully quiet, feeling too foolish even to be mad.

The man in the derby came out again and said that Bubbles would now dance for us. Some thumpy music began playing, and he pulled back the flap and let Bubbles out. We crowded up to the rope.

She was a tall black-haired woman who looked hardmouthed and tired until she faced us and began to smile and sway back and forth to the music. Her eyebrows were painted black and curled around on the ends; where she'd sweated the paint had run down the sides of her face. Her clothes were made of a gauzy red material that you could see through, except for a skimpy brassiere and pants. She was decked out in feathers and jewels, and a silky tassle was fastened to each of her breasts. Mushmouth and Chicken Little were standing next to me. I kept my head turned away from them so they wouldn't recognize me.

Bubbles danced back and forth across the tent a time or two, and then she stopped midway of the rope and stood there smiling, looking at us under her eyebrows. She started the tassle on her right breast twirling around. She stopped that tassle and twirled the other one. After that she twirled both of them at the same time. Everybody whistled and cheered.

"I'm going to teach my old lady to do that," somebody said.

When Bubbles got both tassles going she began to wiggle her hips. Mushmouth looked as if somebody had hit him in the face with a big grin and it had stuck there. He leaned over the rope and started grabbing at Bubbles, and the man in the derby had to come and tell him to behave himself. Chicken Little looked the other way, trying to act like somebody else's twin brother.

Bubbles sashayed across the tent again and went back into her booth. The man in the derby walked out and told us that for fifty cents more we could see Bubbles reveal other secrets of the mysterious East. Nobody liked that, and there was a good deal of cursing and grumbling. But they all shelled out. Brother and I did too. It seemed a shame to leave after we'd all stared at Bubbles and let her begin her show, even if it was wrong to make us pay a dollar for what they'd told us was worth fifty cents.

The music started and Bubbles came back. She wiggled and danced and took off her clothes until she was as naked as a jaybird. With all the jewels and feathers gone she looked the way any ordinary person would look naked, except for the eyebrow paint streaked down the sides of her face. She wasn't as pretty as I'd thought she'd be. It was hard to think of her as the Princess of Mesopotamia, or even somebody named Bubbles. I felt sorry for her then, standing there without her clothes in front of a crowd of men who'd paid a dollar to look at her. It was a cheap thing, and she couldn't grin enough to change it.

Then before anybody could catch him Mushmouth had climbed over the rope and was trying to catch Bubbles. She never did quit dancing. She just skipped from one place to another as nimble as a cat, keeping out of his way, with Mushmouth slobbering and floundering after her, smacking his mouth like a blind dog in a meathouse.

"You come out of there, Mushmouth," Chicken Little said.

Half of the men were whooping for him to get away and leave her alone, and the other half were whooping for him to catch her.

"Go to it, Mushmouth," somebody said.

Chicken Little said, "Mushmouth, you quit that now."

Then the man in the derby caught him and threw him out over the rope. He and Chicken Little went out the door together, hanging their heads. They seemed to get the worst of everything.

The show was over then, and we were happy to get out. It was dinnertime by then and we were hungry. We found a tent where they were selling hamburgers and ate three apiece. Then we went to another tent where a man was selling watermelons and ate four slices apiece for dessert. After that we decided to go and ride the Ferris wheel.

But on the way to the Ferris wheel we passed a tent where some gypsy women were telling fortunes. Three of them were standing in front of the tent, calling to the crowd. One pointed to Brother and me. "You boys are brothers. You let us tell your fortune."

Brother said he didn't want his fortune told and kept walking toward the Ferris wheel. But the youngest of the women ran out and caught my hand.

"You got nice things in your future, handsome boy. Let me tell you about it. For a quarter I will tell you all that will happen to you."

She was pretty, and she sounded like she really needed the money. I gave her a quarter and followed her into the tent. The inside was divided into rooms and we went into one of them. She took my hand and looked into the palm. There was a mole under her left eye and she was wearing a scarf and bright gold earrings.

"I see you will have happiness," she said, "and sorrow, but not as much sorrow as happiness. I see you will have a beautiful wife. I see you will have a lot of money before you are old."

She looked down into my hand again. "I see you will travel. You will see strange parts of the world."

I didn't believe in fortunetelling, but I couldn't help feeling uncomfortable, as if she saw how I looked without my clothes on.

She traced her finger across my hand and said, "From this line I see that you will have a very long life."

That line was a scar from a barbed-wire cut, but I didn't tell her that.

"You are a nice boy," she said. "If you will let me I will bless your money for you. For free. Because I like you." She held out her hand and smiled at me.

I never had heard of that, but I didn't want to hurt her feelings. I got out my pocketbook and handed it to her.

"Now," she said. "You must put your hand on my heart."

She took my hand and put it down inside her dress. She didn't have on any underwear at all. The feeling of her went all through me. I couldn't look at her. She spoke some sort of conjure over my pocketbook and handed it back to me.

After I got away from the tent I looked to see what she'd done to my money when she blessed it. It was gone. Two dollars. She'd stolen it all. And there wasn't a thing to do about it.

I started looking for Brother, edging through the carnival and watching in front of the tents. The crowd was thick. The afternoon was hot and close, and the carnival had begun to have the smell of sweat and cotton candy. Everybody had been there long enough to be tired and bad-tempered. It was miserable. I wished I was at home, a long way from that crowd and the gypsies and the two-headed babies and the Sheik of Araby's wife.

I found Brother playing some sort of game with a mean-looking little man in a checkered shirt. There was a circle of nails driven into the counter of the man's booth, and in the center a wooden arm set on an axle. You bought a red washer for a quarter and put it on one of the nails. The man spun the arm, and if it stopped on your nail you won a dollar. If you bought two washers you stood to win two dollars. When I came up Brother had just laid down a quarter.

"Have you got any money?" I asked him.

"I will have just as soon as he spins this thing again," Brother said. He had eight washers stuck around on the nails.

The man spun the arm and it stopped on a nail that Brother didn't have a washer on.

"That was my last quarter," Brother said.

I had two quarters left and I gave him those. He bought two more washers and tried it again. If he'd won he'd have had eighteen dollars. But he lost. He had a nickel left, but that wasn't enough to buy any more chances, and I was glad of it. We never did get to the Ferris wheel, and I didn't mind that either. I guessed that if we'd paid the dime or quarter or whatever it cost to get on, somebody would have made us pay a dollar to get off.

"Come on," I said. "Let's see how Uncle Burley's doing."

We went back through the crowd to where Uncle Burley had his tank of ducks. People were still waiting to try their luck with the embroidery hoops. Uncle Burley winked at us. His pockets were crammed with the dimes he'd taken in.

We went off to the side and sat under a tree to watch the people try to ring a duck and wait for Uncle Burley to be ready to go home.

It wasn't long until the ducks began to get tired. They'd had a hard day of it, and one after another they quit ducking when the hoops came at them. They just sat there, looking fretful and disgusted and let the people win Uncle Burley's profit. He'd made the throwing line only a few feet from the tank, and everybody began ringing ducks. The people who'd lost in the morning heard what was going on and came back. Uncle Burley's pockets were flattening out fast. He looked more fretful and disgusted than the ducks.

Finally he called Brother and me. He was down to six or seven dollars, and he gave us all but one of them. "Take care of things until I get back," he said. "I won't be a minute."

After Uncle Burley left, Brother stood by the tank to pick the hoops up, and I handled the money. Our first customer was the man in the brown suit who'd lost the bet to Uncle Burley that morning. I could see that he'd come back to get even, and I was afraid he'd make trouble, but he won five dollars on his second throw; that seemed to satisfy him, and he left. But then I was really in a mess; Uncle Burley hadn't come back and I only had eighty cents.

I was wondering what in the world I'd do if somebody else won and found out that I didn't have money enough to pay him, when I saw the head fly off one of the ducks. It couldn't have been done any neater with a butcher knife, but nobody was even close to the tank. I looked over at the shooting gallery, and there was Uncle Burley popping away at the target and ringing the bell every time. Then I saw him lead off toward the ducks as if he were making a wing shot; and another duck flopped in the tank.

When he'd killed all the ducks Uncle Burley walked off toward the other end of the carnival without looking back. He was carrying a big red plaster frog that he'd won at the shooting gallery. Everybody stood around, looking at us and looking at the ducks and looking at Uncle Burley going off through the crowd, with their mouths open. Then they all laughed a little and began to straggle back into the carnival.

I put Uncle Burley's eighty cents in my pocket, and Brother and I started after him.

We caught up with him in front of Bubbles' tent. He and Big Ellis were listening to the man in the derby hat make his speech. We stood with them, listening a while, then Uncle Burley said, "Let's go."

We elbowed our way out of the crowd and Big Ellis went with us.

"I'd like to have a little something to drink," he said to Uncle Burley.

Uncle Burley just carried his red frog and didn't say anything.

Big Ellis said, "I got a little something." He looked at Brother and me and then at Uncle Burley. "It's all right, ain't it?"

"I imagine," Uncle Burley said.

He let Big Ellis take the lead, and we followed him across the grounds to where he'd parked his car. When we got there Big Ellis opened the door and rammed his hand into a hole in the driver's seat and pulled out a pint of whiskey. He said that was the first Fourth of July he'd ever been able to hide it where Annie May couldn't find it.

"She can smell it before it's even uncorked," he said.

He opened the bottle and passed it to Uncle Burley. Uncle Burley set the frog on the seat of the car and drank.

"She couldn't track it inside that seat," Big Ellis said. He giggled and drank out of the bottle when Uncle Burley passed it back to him.

They sat down and leaned against the side of the car, handing the bottle back and forth. Every time Big Ellis took a drink he'd giggle and say something about Annie May's nose not being as good as it used to be.

And the happier Big Ellis got the sadder Uncle Burley got. Those ducks had hurt his feelings and he couldn't get over it.

"God Almighty, women are awful," Big Ellis said, and giggled and wiped the whiskey off his chin.

He hadn't any more than said it before Annie May came around the car, mad as a sow and screeching like a catamount. She told Big Ellis to get himself in that car and take her home. They left with Uncle Burley's red frog sitting bug-eyed on the seat between them.

Uncle Burley stood there with the bottle in his hand and watched them go. Then he drank the rest of the whiskey and threw the bottle down. He swayed back and forth, looking down at it.

"Well," he said, "around and around she goes."

It was dark by the time we got the tank emptied and loaded on the wagon and started home. Brother drove, and Uncle Burley sat on the back of the wagon leaning against the tank. He was quiet all the way.

The moon was up when we turned into Grandpa's gate, shining nearly as bright as day. The river bottom was white and quiet below us, and away off somewhere we could hear a dog barking. It seemed a long time since the Fourth of July.

❧

The next morning Annie May Ellis came over to bring the red frog home, and told Grandma about Uncle Burley's day at the picnic. Grandma told Grandpa and Daddy, and from then on Uncle Burley had no peace. Grandma lit into him about his sinful behavior every chance she got. Grandpa ignored him, but he ignored him in a way that kept all of us from being comfortable when the two of them were together. Even Daddy was aggravated, and that was unusual because he and Uncle Burley had always allowed each other to be the way they were and had got along.

Nobody knew what to do with the red frog. Uncle Burley was too proud to claim it, and Grandpa was too proud to throw it away. Annie May had set it on the mantelpiece in the living room when she came in that morning, and it stayed there. Grandma said she'd just leave it as a reminder to Uncle Burley. But it was a better reminder to her and Grandpa and Daddy than it was to Uncle Burley. He never looked at it.

He was used to that sort of trouble and he stood it well enough. He stayed in a quiet good humor that kept him always a little beyond their reach. But it was intentional good humor; there were times when it was too quiet and too pleasant, and although it spared him a lot of his trouble it could be as insulting as the red frog. He wouldn't say he was sorry and he wouldn't let them make him mad. That kept them after him.

During the week he worked hard. He stood the work the same way he stood everything else, laughing when he could, saying no more than he had to. The work sheltered him; he didn't give them a chance to find fault with him in that. When it was over on Saturday night he ate his supper and left. He'd go to the camp house at the river and stay until Monday morning, avoiding Sunday when Grandma had sin on her mind and Grandpa and Daddy had time enough to be quarrelsome.

While this was going on Brother and I quit being as good friends as we'd always been. I didn't know when it started, but things gradually began to change between us. He started running around with boys who were older than I was, and he went to town every Saturday night. Sometimes I noticed that I called him Tom instead of Brother. I was sorry, but he never gave me a chance to talk about it, and it just kept happening. I spent more time with Uncle Burley; and once in a while I'd walk to the Easterlys' and talk to Calvin. I didn't like Calvin much, but he was about my age, and he was better than nobody.

One Saturday at the end of July, while we were at work in the hay, Big Ellis and Gander Loyd began riding Brother about having a girl in town. I didn't pay much attention to it then. But that evening, after we'd done the chores and Brother had gone upstairs to get ready for town, Grandma said, "Tom's got a girl, hasn't he?"

"I don't know," I said.

"Well, I don't know either. But he's getting old enough. And if I know the signs he's got a girl." She shook her head. "Lord, it seems just yesterday when he was a baby."

She finished straining the milk and went into the kitchen to start supper, and I went to the front porch and sat in the swing. I could hear Uncle

Burley calling his hounds. He whistled and called each one by its name. In the field by the house Grandpa's mules were grazing along the side of the hill. I could see the sweaty marks of the harness on their backs and shoulders. They looked naked and strange without the harness. The day had come apart. After the week of hard work Sunday would feel awkward and too quiet, and even though we were glad of the rest we'd be a little relieved when it was Monday again. I heard the hounds come up to be fed, barking around Uncle Burley until he pitched the food to them, then quiet. A few swifts circled up into the sky and down again over the tops of the chimneys. The mules grazed side by side on the hill, walking together as if they were still at work.

In a little while Brother came around the corner of the house. He'd already eaten his supper and was dressed up, ready to go. His hair was shiny and black from the oil he'd put on it, and I could smell shaving lotion.

"You going to town?" I asked him.

"You got any objections?"

"What're you going to town for?"

He grinned at me, feeling the part in his hair with the ends of his fingers. "You don't know, do you?"

I watched him walk down the driveway and turn toward town. Uncle Burley came up and leaned against the post at the corner of the porch. He'd hunted me up to stay with me until supper was ready; he wouldn't risk being alone with Grandpa even that long. I scooted over and made room for him.

But he stood there, watching Brother walk out the lane. "Where's he going?"

"To town."

"He's courting a little, I expect."

"I don't know," I said.

Uncle Burley sat down. He leaned his head back and yawned and then closed his eyes. "There's one good thing about work," he said.

"What?"

"Stopping."

Grandma called us to supper. We went inside and washed our hands and sat down at the table. It was hot and stuffy in the kitchen, and with

Brother gone the meal was quieter than usual. As long as Uncle Burley was there Grandma and Grandpa wouldn't allow themselves to say anything pleasant, and they seemed too tired to be in a bad humor.

When Grandpa had cleaned his plate he turned his chair to the window and looked out at the sky. "We'll get a rain," he said. "It's been too hot."

He got up after a minute and left the room, and before the rest of us were finished eating we heard him going up the stairs.

"He's gone to roost," Uncle Burley said.

"You've got no respect, Burley," Grandma said.

She'd meant to say more, but held it back. She looked down at her plate, and then got up and began clearing the table.

Uncle Burley and I went to the porch again. He lit a cigarette and sharpened the end of the match to pick his teeth. Neither of us said anything. The day had been hot, and it was still hot. No air was stirring.

Uncle Burley flipped the butt of his cigarette out into the yard. He laughed then — quietly and to himself, as if it were the laughter he'd had ready for whatever Grandma had intended to say to him; and now he used it up, wasted it on himself, to be rid of it.

He got up and stood on the edge of the porch, looking out in the direction of the road. He held his hands open in front of him and looked at them, then rubbed them together. "Well," he said. He stepped off the porch and walked slowly across the yard. Halfway down the driveway he looked back and waved at me. After that he walked faster, on down the driveway and out the lane.

When he was out of sight I called to Grandma that I was going over to see Calvin, and I started through the field toward the Easterlys'. It was nearly dark, but when I looked back the swifts still circled above the house. They dived at the chimney tops, and swerved away as if they couldn't bear for the day to end. Finally, I knew, they'd give up the light and go down for good.

When I got to the Easterlys' I called Calvin from the back door. He came out and we sat down on the step.

"What you been doing?" he asked me.

"Working mostly."

"Where's Tom?"

"Gone to town."

"He's got a girl out there, ain't he?"

"They say he has."

"He has," Calvin said. He took a sack of peppermint sticks out of his pocket and took one and gave one to me.

"Maybe he has," I said.

"What we ought to do," Calvin said, "is slip out to town and watch him."

"It's his business," I said.

"Come on. It won't hurt anything. You'll have something to tell on Tom when you go to work Monday morning."

"All right," I said.

Calvin laughed and stomped his foot. "God durn, I wish I could be there when you tell it on him."

There was a crowd in town. Groups of men squatted on the sidewalk in front of the stores, talking and greeting each other. Up the street beyond the store lights the small children played tag, running and laughing around the parked automobiles. Women collected in the stores and talked while they shopped, and carried out armloads of groceries. A few of them were already standing at the edge of the sidewalk, holding their babies, waiting for their men to be ready to go home. Above the rest of the noise you could hear the jukebox playing in the poolroom.

Brother and four or five other boys were standing with two girls in the light of the drugstore window. He was talking and the others leaned toward him, listening to what he said. The prettiest one of the girls stood next to Brother, smiling at him while he talked, and he spoke mostly to her. She was his girl, I imagined, and I was proud of him for having one so pretty. While I watched him standing there with the other boys it seemed to me that he was the best of them, and I began to be ashamed of what I'd come to town for.

When he finished talking all of them laughed. The girl swung away from him, holding to his hand, and he pulled her back and put his arm around her.

I stood with Calvin, pretending to look in the grocery store window, hoping Brother wouldn't see me. But then the whole bunch of them started up the street past us. I didn't want Brother to know I'd sneaked on him, and I turned toward him to make the best of it.

"Hello," he said. "What're you doing here?"

For a minute I couldn't think what to say. Then I said, "Let's go down to the river and talk to Uncle Burley for a while."

They laughed, looking at Brother and then at me.

"Go ahead," Brother told me. "Who's stopping you?"

The way he said it made me mad. "I reckon you'd rather stay here and fool around with a damn girl," I said.

Brother's face got red and he took a step toward me, but the girl pulled at his arm. "Come on," she said.

He looked at me and laughed, then he turned around and they went past me and on up the street.

I stood still for a minute, feeling my own face red and knowing I'd made a fool of myself. There was no other way to see it. What I'd said had been wrong. Brother ought to have slapped my face for saying it. And I thought I should have knocked Calvin's teeth out for suggesting that we come to town in the first place. I turned to tell him so, but he was gone. I looked around for him and saw him going into the drugstore. He was ashamed of me too.

I started back down the street. The game had moved down in front of the stores, the children chasing each other in and out of the crowd. As I walked away I heard a woman's voice telling them, "Get someplace else if you want to play."

I went out the road toward home, feeling lonesome and stupid and ashamed. For a while I could hear the noise of the town, the music and talking and laughter, more quietly and more quietly as I got farther away. The frogs were singing in Big Ellis's pond when I passed, the sounds getting louder and then quieting too. I turned into our lane, but I didn't feel like going to bed and I went on past the house and down Coulter Branch toward the river. Now and then I'd hear a screech owl calling, and now and then a dog barked down in the bottom.

When I got to Uncle Burley's shack a light was burning in the window. I opened the door and went through the dark kitchen and into the other room where Uncle Burley and Big Ellis were sitting with a bottle of whiskey and a lighted lamp on the table between them. Their backs were turned to the kitchen door, and Uncle Burley had pulled one of the cots away from the wall and propped his feet on it. When Big Ellis looked around and saw me he started to hide the bottle, but Uncle Burley caught his arm and stopped him.

"It's all right."

"He's a good boy, that boy is," Big Ellis said.

Uncle Burley grinned at me. "The more the merrier," he said. "Have a seat."

I crossed the room and sat down on the other cot.

"Where you been, boy?" Uncle Burley asked me.

"I went to town a while," I said, "and then I came down here."

"I'm glad you came," Uncle Burley said.

"He's a pretty damn good boy, I tell you," Big Ellis said.

Neither of them could think of anything else to say. They just smoked, and passed the bottle once in a while, looking at the wall.

Finally Uncle Burley said, "It's hot."

"It's too hot," Big Ellis said. "We're bound to get some rain."

They were quiet again for a minute or two, and then Uncle Burley looked at Big Ellis and grinned as if he'd just thought of something that made him happy.

"I wonder if old Jig's at home," he said.

Big Ellis leaned toward the window and looked up the river toward Jig Pendleton's shanty boat. "No light up there. I expect he's asleep."

"The more the merrier," Uncle Burley said. He got up and went out the door.

Big Ellis and I followed him onto the porch. Jig's boat was dark and quiet. We could barely make out the shape of it through the trees.

"Call him," Big Ellis said.

Uncle Burley cupped his hands around his mouth and called, "Jig!"

There was no answer.

"Call him again," Big Ellis said; and Uncle Burley called again.

"What?" Jig said.

"Come on down," Uncle Burley said. "We're having a little social event here."

Jig didn't answer, but before long he came out with a lantern and untied his rowboat. We heard the knock and creak of his oarlocks as he came down the river toward us.

Jig tied the boat to a tree and climbed the bank. When he came onto the porch we went back inside and he followed us.

"How're you, Jig?" Uncle Burley asked.

Jig blew out his lantern and hung it on a nail over the door, and then he shook our hands. I'd never seen anybody look so sad in my life.

"No man's strength is equal to his wickedness," he said. "God has to forgive us before he can love us. Surely the people is grass."

"The more the merrier, Jig," Uncle Burley said. "Have a seat."

Jig sat down. Big Ellis handed him the bottle and he drank.

"That's an evil thing, Burley," he said. He looked at the bottle and handed it to Uncle Burley.

"But ain't it a mellow-ripe sample of it?" Uncle Burley said.

Jig shook his head. "Mellow as sin, Burley, and ripe."

Uncle Burley looked at him and then patted his shoulder. "You'll feel better when it's morning, old Jig."

Uncle Burley and Big Ellis sat down and began drinking again. But Jig had made them sad and they were even quieter than they'd been before. The three of them passed the bottle back and forth, drinking as if it were a chore they'd be glad to be done with.

Their seriousness and quietness began to bother me. I was more in the dumps than I'd been when I got there. I wished I'd gone on home to bed.

"I'd just as soon it was morning," Uncle Burley said.

"I'd just as soon it was," Big Ellis said.

"What time is it?"

Big Ellis got out his watch and held it to the light. "Half past eleven."

"She's a slow one, ain't she?" Uncle Burley said. Then he said, "Wind that thing."

Big Ellis wound the watch and put it back in his pocket.

Jig got up and wobbled out the door, and I heard him take his boots off and lie down on the porch. Uncle Burley and Big Ellis didn't seem to notice he was gone. I leaned back against the wall and dozed off. But I couldn't get all the way to sleep; every little sound woke me. Sometimes

I'd hear Jig turning over on the porch. He'd grunt and say, "Oh me," and then be quiet again. And Uncle Burley and Big Ellis sat on, drinking at the table.

Finally I heard Big Ellis say, "Where's Jig?"

"I don't know," Uncle Burley said. "We ought to get him to come and talk to us."

"Tell him to," Big Ellis said.

Uncle Burley stood up, and then he got down on his hands and knees and began crawling toward the door.

Big Ellis giggled. "What're you crawling for?"

"You got to watch this floor," Uncle Burley said. "It's a booger."

He got to the door and called, "Oh, Jig!"

Jig stirred and grunted. "What?"

"Come on down, Jig. We got a little social event going on here."

"All right," Jig said.

Uncle Burley cocked his ear up the river and listened.

"Is he coming?" Big Ellis asked.

"No," Uncle Burley said. "I can't even see a light."

"He'll come," Big Ellis said. "Call him again."

Uncle Burley called, "Jig!"

I heard one of Jig's elbows thump on the porch.

"What?"

"Come on."

"All right."

Uncle Burley listened again.

"You hear him yet?" Big Ellis asked.

"Aw, he ain't coming," Uncle Burley said. "He's scared of the dark." He stretched out across the doorway and folded his hands over his chest. "We'll see him in the morning, I reckon."

When I looked back at Big Ellis he was asleep, his head resting against the tabletop. They seemed to have settled down for the night. I was too sleepy to go home, so I took off my shoes and stretched out on the cot, thinking I'd take a nap and then get home before daylight to keep from worrying Grandma.

When I woke it was thundering. A strong wind had come up,

fluttering the lamp flame until the whole house seemed to sway and jiggle in the wind. The rest of them were still asleep. Big Ellis hadn't moved since I'd lain down. The light bobbled his shadow over the wall behind him, and when the lightning flashes came his shadow jumped to the other wall and flickered there. It was like waking up on Judgment Day.

I was trying to untangle the blanket to pull it over my head when the rain came — a few big drops spattered the roof, and then a sheet of water blew into the door where Uncle Burley was sleeping.

He rolled over. "Quit," he said. He wiped the water out of his eyes and scrambled into the room. Jig followed him in and slammed the door.

Big Ellis sat up and rubbed his eyes. "It's raining," he said.

"You ought to been a prophet," Uncle Burley said. He sat down at the table again.

The lightning got worse. Jig stood in the middle of the floor and watched it, as wild-eyed as a ghost.

"Burley," he said, "He could strike us down with one of them."

"I reckon so," Uncle Burley said.

"He could strike you down just like a rabbit."

"He can shoot 'em like a rifle," Uncle Burley said.

It lightened again; the thunder clapped down, jarring the house.

"Oh," Jig said. He fell on the floor with his hands over his face.

"Bull's-eye," Uncle Burley said.

The thunder bumbled away over the top of the hill.

"Burley, that one struck something," Big Ellis said.

"It must have," Uncle Burley said.

We went to the windows and looked out, but it was raining too hard to see anything. Jig was still on the floor hiding his face.

"Get up, Jig," Uncle Burley said. "You're not dead."

He and Big Ellis helped Jig onto his feet.

"He ain't even wounded," Big Ellis said.

Jig sat down on one of the cots and put his hands over his face again. "Burley, He let me live. And He didn't have to do it. He didn't have any reason to do it. It was out of his goodness. He don't have to stand for any such foolishness, Burley."

The rain didn't last long. When it was over we went out on the porch to see if we could tell what the lightning had struck. The stars were shining where the cloud had passed, and everything was cool and fresh-smelling. I felt as wide awake as if I'd slept all night.

Big Ellis went around the corner of the house, and then we heard him say, "Burley, yonder's a fire."

"Where?" Uncle Burley asked him. He went around the house, and Jig and I hurried after him.

Big Ellis pointed. "Right up there."

We saw the smoke beginning to roll up over the top of the hill, and under it the dim red shimmer of the fire.

"It's at our place," I said.

"It could be," Uncle Burley said.

He started toward the road and Big Ellis went with him. Jig had gone back to the porch to put his boots on, and I ran into the house to get my shoes. Jig waited for me at the door, and then we started after the others. We ran hard and caught up with them a little past Beriah Easterly's store.

The trees hid the smoke from us, but by the time we were halfway up the hill we heard a bell ringing.

"That's the dinner bell," Uncle Burley said.

He broke into a run, and the rest of us strung out behind him. I could hear Jig's rubber boots bumping and stumbling behind me.

We were out of breath when we got up on the ridge and we slowed to a walk. But by that time we could see that the fire was in Daddy's barn, and we only walked a few steps before we started running again.

When we went past Grandpa's house Grandma was standing in the yard in her nightgown, ringing the dinner bell. She waved and called something to us.

Uncle Burley slowed down. "What?"

"Buckets!" she said. "Get some buckets."

We ran to the back porch and got the milk bucket and the slop bucket and the two water buckets. When we ran back into the yard she was ringing the bell again. She called something else to us when we went past her, but we didn't stop to hear what she said. She was barefooted, the firelight red on her face and gown.

Daddy's team had been in the barn, and he and Grandpa had got them out and turned them loose in the lot. The two mules stood together in the farthest corner, their heads up, turning to face the fire, then snorting and whirling away.

Daddy and Grandpa were dipping water out of the trough at the well and carrying it into the driveway where part of the loft had broken through. The fire had started in the far end of the barn, and the wind seemed to be holding it back a little.

When we got into the lot Jig stopped and pointed at the fire. "That's what it's like," he said. "The fire of Hell, my brothers in sin." Then he grabbed the pump handle and began pumping.

We stood in line to fill our buckets, and carried them into the barn and emptied them. Grandpa and Daddy had set the pace, and we kept it up, running from the well to the fire and back again. The driveway was so full of smoke that we could hardly breathe or see. I held my breath and ran in until I could see the light of the fire, and flung the bucket of water at it and ran out again, coughing and wiping my eyes while I waited in line at the well.

"It's got too much of a start," Uncle Burley said. "We'll never stop it."

I knew he told the truth. It had been hopeless when we got there. But he never stopped or slowed down, and none of the rest of us did either.

A crowd had gathered at the yard fence. The red light flickered and waved on their faces, and shone on the roofs of the automobiles behind them. Their faces looked calm and strange turned up into the light of the fire, like the faces of people around a lion's cage, separate from it, only seeing.

And once when I came back to the well with my empty bucket I saw that Brother was standing in the line ahead of me. Gander Loyd and Beriah Easterly and Mr. Feltner had come to help us too. But it was hopeless. Nothing was there to save, only a thing to look at. Grandma still rang the dinner bell, but we couldn't hear it now above the sound of the fire. Jig worked at the pump.

For a few minutes we managed to hold the fire at the back of the driveway. But it was spreading into the loft, and there was nothing we could do about that. Finally the heat drove us outside. The driveway ticked and cracked like an oven, and then the whole barn blazed up at once. Flames shot over the well top and we dropped our buckets and ran. We stood in the center of the lot, watching the fire and getting our breath.

"You all haven't got any barn," Gander said. "You've just got a fire." He turned around and walked toward the crowd at the fence.

Beriah stood with us for another minute or two, and then shook his head. "It's gone now." He followed Gander away.

Daddy never looked at them, nor at any of us. He watched the fire die down after the first big blaze; and when the wind turned the flames back from the well he moved toward the barn again, without looking back or asking us to go with him, and without any hope, but going anyway. Grandpa started after him, hurrying to catch up. Uncle Burley and Big Ellis and Mr. Feltner and Brother and Jig and I followed them.

Jig ran past us and splashed water on the pump handle to cool it, and pumped again. We filled our buckets and began dowsing the wall nearest the pump. Daddy wet his clothes so he could get closer to the fire, and we passed our buckets to him. He was furious, throwing water at the fire as if he were trying to bruise it. We worked to keep the fire away from the pump, and to save the crib and the granary and the wagon shed. Cinders dropped on our faces and hands, and scorched our clothes; we brushed them off and kept going. Jig worked the pump with his whole body, rattling the handle up and down as if he were doing some kind of dance.

Big Ellis yelled, "Look out!" and we ran again.

We ran to the fence and turned around in time to see the whole barn cave in — loft and roof and walls — like logs in a fireplace. Red ashes spewed around it on the ground; sparks from the hay spiraled and wound into the smoke.

We went back to the well again. From then on we worked more slowly, but we never stopped. Daddy and Grandpa kept us going. They hated the fire and they had to fight it, and none of us would leave them to fight it alone. We stayed with them, and we saved the outbuildings.

By morning the fire was out. We left our buckets at the well and went into the lot and sat down. We were too worn out to try to talk. We were blackened and parched and blistered, our eyes bloodshot and stinging from the smoke.

While daylight came we sat and looked at the black pile of ashes. We hadn't accepted the fire; we'd been able to fight that as long as it burned. But now, in the daylight, in our tiredness, as if we'd fought all night in a dream, we accepted the ashes.

It was quiet. The crowd had gone soon after the barn caved in, and Grandma had long ago quit ringing the bell. At the far end of the lot the two mules grazed on the short grass. After a while they walked over to the trough at the well, and Jig got up and pumped water for them.

"Bless you, God's creatures," he said.

They drank, and then Daddy opened the gate and turned them out on the hillside.

Uncle Burley found the drinking cup where it had been kicked into the ashes. Jig rinsed it and filled it for each of us and we drank. Daddy was the last to drink; when he finished he turned the cup upside down and set it carefully beside the base of the pump. After that there seemed to be nothing to do.

❧

After the fire Uncle Burley quit leaving home on the weekends. He could be free with his own troubles but not with Daddy's. He did his best to be agreeable; and with the loss of the barn to worry about, everybody seemed to have forgotten how he'd misbehaved on the Fourth of July.

One day he carried the red frog to Big Ellis's house and asked Annie May to accept it as a gift from a friend. There was nothing she could do but take it and thank him.

Several weeks went by before we cleaned up the ruins of the barn. The black pile of ruck and cinders was too dismal. Daddy hated the sight of it; and I knew it was hard for him to think of cleaning it up, as if that would only finish what the fire had begun. After the swiftness of the fire I felt the ashes would stay forever.

But finally one Friday morning all of us went to work and hauled away the leavings. Once we'd got beyond our dread of the job we were anxious to be rid of every trace of the fire.

Brother stayed mad at me for what I'd said to him in town the night the barn burned. I'd been in the wrong, and he never gave me a chance to forget it.

On the Saturday night after we'd cleared away the remainders of the old barn Calvin came over to our house. I hadn't seen him since he'd slipped away from me in town, and I didn't care if I never saw him again. But when I went out of the house that night, after we'd finished supper and Brother had left for town, Calvin was coming across the yard.

He grinned at me, sucking on a peppermint stick. "What're you doing?"

I didn't go to meet him. "I'm standing here looking at you," I said.

He came on across the yard and sat down. I walked away toward the barn, and he got up again and followed me.

"Want some candy?" he asked.

"No thanks."

"Let's do something."

He trailed along behind me. I heard him close the sack and put it back in his pocket.

"I'm walking out to the barn," I said, "and I don't need your help."

"Let's go down to the river and talk to Uncle Burley for a while," he said, mocking the way I'd said it to Brother.

I turned on him and he dodged. I waited until he looked at me, and then I grinned. "Give me a stick of candy," I said.

He held the sack out and I helped myself.

"Let's go and see how Brother's getting along with his courting," I said.

He looked away. "We'd better not do that."

"Come on," I told him.

I started toward the road. He stood there a minute and then hurried after me. When we got to the road he caught up and walked beside me into town.

Brother and his girl were drinking Cokes at one of the tables in the back of the drugstore. We stood in front and watched them through the window until they got up and started out.

"We'd better get out of sight," Calvin said.

We crossed the street to the churchyard and watched them leave the drugstore. The moon had come up, but the trees around the church made shadow enough to hide us.

"Let's follow them," I said.

"We oughtn't to do that."

I told him to quit being such a chicken, and he didn't say any more.

We let them get a long way off, then followed. They went along the road toward the river, walking slowly with their arms around each other. When we'd got beyond the noise of the town we could hear Brother talking—the rising and falling of his voice, too quiet for us to make out the words. And now and then the girl laughed. Sometimes when she laughed she laid her head on Brother's shoulder.

Calvin nudged me in the ribs. "Look at that. Wait till you tell Tom you saw that." He had another peppermint stick in his mouth.

We passed the graveyard and I could see the angel on the Coulter monument standing up black over the tops of the trees. Brother and the girl walked close together. The moon threw their shadows behind them on the road.

They turned off where the road started down to the river and went along a path to a level place on the hillside. We stopped behind a bush at a bend in the path where we could look down on them.

"God durn if this ain't some fun," Calvin said.

The girl sat down and held her hand out to Brother, and he sat down beside her. She took the scarf off and put it in her purse, then ran her fin-gers through her hair and let it fall back over her shoulders. She reached and touched Brother's face. The light on her hair moved when she moved. Brother put his arms around her and kissed her. I looked at Calvin. He was standing there with his mouth open, watching them as if it were happening in a picture show. I jerked his sleeve to tell him to come on, and went up to the road again.

Before long Calvin came up opening the sack of peppermint sticks. He was grinning. "We've sure got a good one on old Tom now. You wait till we tell it on him."

"You'd better not," I said.

He looked at me. "Why?"

I caught him by the collar and shoved him backward. The peppermint sticks shook out all over the road.

"God damn you, go home."

I shoved him again, and he ran until he was out of sight over the hill.

I went on toward home then, and where our lane turned off I stopped and waited. There was nobody on the road. All the houses I'd passed were dark and quiet.

I heard Brother's footsteps. And then I could see him. When he saw me he took his hands out of his pockets and walked faster.

"What're you doing here?" His voice sounded peaceful and friendly.

"Just messing around."

"Well, let's go home." He started into the lane.

"Tom," I said. "I saw you."

He turned around. "Saw who?"

"You and that girl. Down there on the hillside."

He hit me square in the face and I fell. My head hit the road.

His footsteps went away and it got quiet again. I felt the blood running out of my mouth.

❦

Brother never mentioned what had happened that Saturday night, and he was peaceable enough afterwards. But he wasn't friendly. He kept his distance. We got along better than I'd expected we would. I had to be grateful for the distance. If we'd been any closer, or tried to be brothers the way we'd always been, we'd have had to keep fighting each other. But we'd quit being brothers, and it was my fault.

When the work let up early in September and Uncle Burley suggested that he and I go fishing for a few days, I was glad of the chance to get away.

We'd been busier than usual during the last part of the summer, and all of us were tired. The weather had been wet, and Daddy and Grandpa hadn't been able to plan work more than a day ahead. That had kept them on edge and hurrying, and Grandpa's patience had worn out.

When we sat down to breakfast that morning Grandpa noticed one of the kitchen windows was shut. He told Grandma to open it.

"It's stuck," she said. "The damp weather made it swell."

"Get up and open the window," Grandpa told Brother.

Brother got up and tried to open it, but it wouldn't budge. Grandma came to help him. But it was stuck tight, and they only got in each other's way.

Grandpa watched them fumbling at the sash for a minute; and then without saying a word he unhooked his cane from the back of his chair and knocked out the glass.

Grandma and Brother dodged the splinters, and Brother sat down again. Grandma stood still for a minute looking at Grandpa, her eyes snapping. But he'd turned his back to her and begun eating. She went to the stove then and took the biscuits out of the oven. We ate without talking or looking at each other.

Grandpa finished in a hurry and went to the barn. Uncle Burley looked at the broken window and the pieces of glass on the floor and began laughing. He looked up at the ceiling and rocked back and forth in his chair, whooping and howling with laughter until Grandpa must have heard it at the barn. He'd stop for a second to get his breath, then he'd look at the window and say "Oh my God" and start laughing again.

"You're a fine one to be laughing," Grandma told him. "It's no funnier than some of the things you do."

He looked at her, still laughing, and said, "Oh my God."

She left the room then, and Uncle Burley quit laughing. He looked across the table at me and said, "Let's go fishing, for God's sake."

I said that suited me but I was afraid Grandpa had work for me to do, and I didn't want to ask him because of the mood he was in.

"I'll take care of that," Uncle Burley said.

Grandpa was harnessing his team in the driveway of the barn. He hadn't told us what he was going to do that day, but nearly always when we had a break in our regular work he'd slip away from us and spend a day or two at odd jobs around the farm — mowing weeds or mending a fence. He liked to work by himself, and he was always resentful if we asked where he was going or offered to help him.

Uncle Burley went into the barn and squatted in the middle of the driveway so that Grandpa had to walk around him. "What're you fixing to do?" he asked.

Grandpa didn't pay any attention to him. He threw the harness over the back of the second mule and buckled it on. He picked up his cane and led the mules out into the lot and began hitching them to the wagon. Uncle Burley got up and followed him.

"You've got the lead mule hitched too short."

"I was working mules before you were born," Grandpa said.

"Well," Uncle Burley said, "Nathan and I think we'll go fishing for a few days."

Grandpa said he didn't give a damn if we fished the rest of the year, and Uncle Burley said he hadn't thought about that but we might do it.

He sent me to the house to tell Grandma we were going. Then we went to the smokehouse and got a side of bacon and a tin can full of salt.

It was a fine brisk morning, cool and bright, the wind in the north. The leaves on some of the bushes beside the road had begun to turn yellow. I knew we wouldn't think of summer again; it was easier to imagine cold and fire in the stoves and snow.

When we came over the brow of the hill we stopped and looked down at the river. The corn in the bottoms had ripened and turned brown; the tobacco patches were naked now that the crop had been put in. The river lay green and quiet between the rows of trees.

"Poor old Chicken Little," Uncle Burley said.

I turned to look at him; he stood there watching the river as if he didn't realize he'd spoken aloud.

Chicken Little Montgomery had fallen out of a boat and drowned the week before, but this was the first time I'd heard any of our family mention it. None of us had ever been friends with the Montgomerys, and we'd never spoken of them. But now that Chicken Little was dead you noticed the silence. All of us felt uneasy about his drowning. He stayed on our minds as if our dislike for him while he was alive had somehow made us guilty of his death.

"Wonder if they've ever found his body," Uncle Burley said.

"I don't know," I said.

We went on down the hill, and up the bottom to Beriah Easterly's store.

Beriah and Gander Loyd were sitting on nail kegs in front of the store, looking up toward the top of the hill. Beriah saw us coming and called, "Morning, Burley."

"Morning, Beriah," Uncle Burley said. "Morning, Gander. I hear you got married."

"It's a fact," Gander said.

Beriah pointed up at the top of the hill. "A lot of buzzards up there this morning. Must be something dead."

We looked at the buzzards for a minute. Then Uncle Burley and I went into the store and Beriah got up and came in after us. He went behind the counter and propped his elbows on it, waiting to hear what we wanted.

Uncle Burley ordered two pounds of line and a hundred hooks, five pounds of meal and three sacks of Bull Durham.

"Going to do some fishing, are you, Burley?" Beriah said when he came back with the line and hooks.

"Thinking about it," Uncle Burley told him.

"Pity about Chicken Little, wasn't it?" Beriah said.

"It was," Uncle Burley said.

"You know they never found his body. They gave him up."

Beriah sacked up the things we'd bought and handed the sack across the counter to me. "Looks like we're going to have some more fishing weather."

"Could be," Uncle Burley said.

"Well, I hope you all have luck."

Gander was still sitting on the nail keg when we came out. Uncle Burley nodded to him. "Give my respects to your wife, Gander."

"Thank you, Burley," Gander said. He got up and went into the store.

When we were on the road again Uncle Burley said, "Gander's out awfully bright and early for a bridegroom."

"I didn't know he was married," I said. "Who did he marry?"

"Old Gander outdid himself, from what I hear. They say he married a young woman. And a pretty one too. Her name was Mandy something or other."

When we got to the camp house Uncle Burley shoved the door open and we went inside. "Well, here we are," he said.

He told me to open the windows, and he got a broom and swept the floors. We took the bedding down and spread it over the beds. After we got everything clean and in order we sat outside to talk and look at the river. There was a breeze blowing and a few spots of sunlight came through the leaves onto the porch; it was quiet and comfortable. We'd gone a few days without rain and the river had cleared, although there was still some current. It felt good to have nothing to do but be there.

"I don't see how Gander ever persuaded a pretty woman to marry him," Uncle Burley said. "That one-eyed old pup. She must be blind in both eyes. I wonder if she's looked at him yet."

"He's not very pretty, " I said.

Uncle Burley laughed. "His face would stop an eight-day clock and run it backwards two weeks."

He lay down on his back and pulled his hat over his eyes. After a minute he laughed again. "Your grandpa sure did ventilate the kitchen," he said. "Damned if he can't be outrageous sometimes."

"It's hard on Grandma," I said.

"And everybody else," Uncle Burley said. He sat up and put his hat back on, folding his arms across his knees. "But I tell you, there's no give in him. And no quit. You've got to admire that. He's been a wheel horse in his time. He's worked like the world was on fire and nobody but him to put it out. It's a shame to see him getting old."

I nodded. Grandpa had been hard on all of us. He'd kept himself stubborn and lonely, not allowing any of us to know him; we saw him and he saw us through his loneliness. But his loneliness and stubborness humbled us too. We had to admire him.

At dinnertime Uncle Burley lit the coal oil stove, and I filled the water bucket at the spring behind the house. We fried some bacon and a pile of corn bread and sat down to eat.

Uncle Burley raised his hat and said,

> "Oh Lord, make us able
> To eat all that's on this table,
> And if there's some we haven't got
> Bring it to us while it's hot."

After dinner we found the boat where Uncle Burley had hidden it in a patch of horseweeds and turned it over and slid it down the bank to the river. And then we got the bait box and the fish box from under the porch and tied them in the river by the boat.

We climbed the bank again and sat on the edge of the porch to rest.

"Well," Uncle Burley said, "we got her fixed. We're in business."

When we'd rested Uncle Burley said we'd better be thinking about catching some bait if we were going to fish. He said there ought to be plenty of perch up in the creek, and we could try them for a start. He found the minnow seine and I got a five-gallon bucket from under the stove in the kitchen. We started upstream toward the mouth of the creek.

Uncle Burley carried the seine on his shoulder, whistling a tune and watching the river.

"Do you think we'll catch any fish?" I asked him.

"The river's full of them," he said. "We ought to. If we get another rain to stir the water and freshen it a little, we ought to have good fishing."

We caught a bucketful of perch up in the creek and carried them back and put them in the bait box at the river. It was getting late by then. Uncle Burley said there wasn't much use in trying to fish that day, so we made another meal off the bacon and corn bread.

As soon as supper was over we set a lantern on the table in the bedroom and started getting our fishing gear in shape. We rolled the hanks of line into balls so they'd run out without tangling when we put them in the river. Uncle Burley got out a ball of lighter line and we snooded the hooks, cutting the line into pieces about a foot and a half long and tying the hooks to them.

It was comfortable work to do after supper. We were full and a little sleepy. A couple of owls called in the woods. Frogs were singing.

The next morning we finished breakfast by sunup. We loaded the lines and hooks and a baiting of perch into the boat and started up the river. Uncle Burley rowed. The red sunlight slanted through the trees on the bank and down to the water. A soft wind was coming up the river, rippling it, and the reflections of the trees were speckled and pointed in the water like big fish. Two or three herons flew from one snag to another, keeping ahead of us. We went past Jig's boat, but it was quiet and we didn't call him.

When we got to the bend where Uncle Burley wanted to fish I tied the end of one of the lines to a willow, and let it unwind as Uncle Burley rowed across to the other bank. We found another willow on that side and fastened the line, then tied on the weights — a small rock near each shore and one in the middle. We pulled ourselves back across on the line, and I tied on the hooks and Uncle Burley baited them.

The sun was getting hot when we finished putting the lines out. Uncle Burley said it would save a lot of rowing if we stayed there for the rest of the morning; we'd run the lines at noon and maybe get a mess of fish, and then go in. He pulled the boat into the shade along the bank and we tied up to a snag.

We made ourselves comfortable and watched the river, talking about how many fish we might catch and what kind and how big. Uncle Burley remembered all the good ones he'd ever caught and what he'd caught them on and what time of year it had been. Finally we ran out of talk, and he lay down in the bottom of the boat and went to sleep.

I watched the sun climb up toward the top of the sky. A few birds were singing, and I could see a mud turtle sunning himself on a log. Kingfishers flew over the willows, calling, tilting down to the water after minnows. After a while it got hotter and the river quieted down. The only things moving then were the clouds and the water.

The surface of the river was still. You could see every leaf of the trees reflected in it. The white glare of the sun glanced so brightly it hurt your eyes; and in the shade where we rested the water darkened, rippling a little as it passed the boat. The whole calm of the river moved down and past us and on, as if it slept and remembered its direction in its sleep. And somewhere below the thin reflections of the trees was Chicken Little, hidden in that dark so quietly nobody would ever find him.

After a while I propped my back against the side of the boat and went to sleep too.

It was nearly noon when Uncle Burley woke me. We ran the lines and took off four or five little catfish, and then rowed back to the house to cook them for dinner.

That afternoon we caught another bucketful of perch, and ran the lines again after it began to cool off. We took six nice channel cats on that run and baited the lines up fresh. Three of the fish made enough for our supper, and we put the other three in the fish box to keep them alive.

It began to rain at supper time, a slow drizzle at first, then hard and steady against the roof and windowpanes. It sounded as if it had set in for the night. When supper was over we sat in the bedroom and talked and listened to the rain fall.

I'd about made up my mind to go to bed when Uncle Burley picked up the lantern and put his hat on. "I feel my luck working," he said. "Let's go see what we've caught."

"At this time of night?" I said.

We waited until the rain slacked up a little, and went down to the boat. It was dark. The rain fell out of the black sky and splattered our clothes and sizzled on the lantern globe. Uncle Burley set the lantern in the front of the boat and we shoved off. We stayed in close under the trees. The lower branches caught in our light and we guided by them.

We ran the first line and took off two white cats and three channel cats, all of a good size. I rowed to the other line and Uncle Burley began raising it. We went about fifteen feet from the bank and I saw the line jerk in his hands. It pulled him off balance and he turned the line loose and caught himself on the other side of the boat.

He wiped his hands on his pants and looked at me. "We got a fish, boy."

"Can you tell how big?"

"Pretty near too big."

I rowed to the bank. He caught the line again, and I held the lantern up so he could see. The line tightened in his hands, cutting back and forth through the water. It was still raining, and pitch-dark beyond the light of the lantern. Uncle Burley knelt in the front of the boat, working us slowly toward the fish. He had his underlip in his teeth, being careful.

We heard the fish roll up on top of the water, his big tail splashing out in the dark toward the middle of the river. He went down then, and Uncle Burley had to turn the line loose. We played the fish for what seemed an hour, running out, losing the line, and rowing back to the bank to start all over again.

Finally we wore him out. He came to the top of the water, and Uncle Burley held him there and pulled the boat out to him. He was a white cat, the biggest I'd ever seen. Uncle Burley hooked his thumb into the fish's mouth and ran the fingers of his other hand into the gills. I caught the tail and we hauled him over the side of the boat. He flopped down at our feet and lay there with his big red gills heaving open and shut. Uncle Burley was breathing hard, and the thumb he'd hooked in the fish's mouth was bleeding. He sat down and looked at the fish while he got his breath, then he grinned at me. "He's a horse, ain't he?"

We were drenched with rain, and by the time we got back to the house our teeth were chattering. We stripped off our clothes and hung them on the chairs to dry. Uncle Burley lit the stove and we stood in front of it until we were warm. When we went to bed the rain was still coming down, rustling through the trees and rapping the tin roof. We lay snug and awake for a long time, remembering everything that had happened.

※

After breakfast the next morning we went down to the river. We'd tied the fish to the back of the boat with a piece of strong line, doubled and looped through one of his gills. Uncle Burley lifted him out of the water. We were surprised again to see how big he was.

"What're we going to do with him?" I asked.

"We'll get Beriah to put him on ice for us so he'll keep," Uncle Burley said. "You can cut slabs of meat off of him as big as steaks, and just as white as snow."

When we'd finished looking at the fish Uncle Burley let him back into the water so he could breathe. He jerked his head against the line like a horse jerking against a hitch rein.

"There'll be a lot of fine eating on that fish," Uncle Burley said. "We ought to have a fish fry. We'll get Big Ellis and Jig and Gander to come down tonight and have a feast. We'll have to let Beriah in on it too, so he'll be willing to furnish some ice."

As soon as we'd baited the lines we took the fish out of the water again. We tied him to one of the oars and started up the road, carrying him between us, holding him high to keep his tail from dragging.

"We'll cook plenty of corn bread," Uncle Burley said, "and maybe get hold of a watermelon. It'll be a supper they won't forget for a while."

Beriah was sitting in front of the store again, and when he saw us he came out to meet us. "Lord amercy," he said. "Look what a fish."

"We're going to use him for bait," Uncle Burley said. "We're going to try to catch one big enough to eat."

Beriah held the door open for us and we carried the fish inside and stretched him out on the floor in front of the counter.

"Lord amercy," Beriah said. "You've caught the granddaddy of them all." He knelt down beside the fish and patted its head as if it were a dog. "You don't see a fish like this more than once in a lifetime, Burley."

When I saw how Beriah admired our fish I was prouder than ever and so was Uncle Burley.

"Don't it make your mouth water just to look at him?" Uncle Burley said.

"There's some fine eating on him, all right," Beriah said.

"I'll tell you what," Uncle Burley said. "We'll clean him and you can put him on ice for us, and then we'll all get together tonight and have a big fish fry."

"Nothing could suit me any better," Beriah said. "But, Burley, you all don't want to dress that fish yet. Keep him a while so people can see him."

They looked at the fish. Uncle Burley leaned over and picked up the line again and held it, as if he were going to lead the fish out of the store.

"He'll spoil."

"No, he won't. We'll keep him alive. Hell, Burley, you don't want to treat him like an ordinary fish. People don't get a chance to see a fish like that every day."

Beriah went to the back of the store and opened the cooler. "Bring a couple of those crates," he said.

He began to take the bottles out of the cooler and we brought the crates and helped him.

"Now, what's the matter with that, Burley? He'll stay alive a long time in that cold water."

"I reckon he will," Uncle Burley said.

Beriah picked up the fish. "Lord amercy," he said.

We helped him lift the fish into the cooler, and then we stood there looking in.

"Why, that's a regular aquarium," Beriah said. "I just wish it had glass sides on it."

Uncle Burley laughed. "Well, we could caulk up the candy counter and put him in that."

Beriah and I laughed too, and we looked at the fish again.

"Well, he looks comfortable enough," Uncle Burley said. He shut the lid and turned around. "We'll be seeing you, Beriah."

Beriah sat down on the bench beside the cooler. "Aw, stick around a while, Burley."

Uncle Burley didn't say whether he'd stay or not, but I could see that he was relieved when Beriah asked him to. He opened the screen door and started out.

"When did you all catch him, Burley?"

Uncle Burley stopped and turned around. "Last night." He stepped back inside and let the door close behind him.

"Last night?" Beriah said. "You all caught a fish like that in the dark?"

"Well," Uncle Burley said, "it wasn't a lot of trouble."

Beriah kept asking questions; and while Uncle Burley answered them he moved back into the store. He walked to the counter, and to the cooler again, and finally sat down on the bench with Beriah and propped up his feet. He'd tell only as much as Beriah asked for, and then he'd wait for another question.

"And what did you do then?" Beriah would ask. And when Uncle Burley told him, he'd let his hands drop onto his knees and say, "Well, I'll swear."

When Uncle Burley began to tell how we'd fought the fish out in the dark and the rain his voice got tight and excited in spite of all he could do. He sounded like somebody was tickling his feet.

Before he got it all told Gander Loyd came in.

"Gander, go look there in the cooler," Beriah said.

"What for?"

"Just go look in it."

Uncle Burley straightened up and Beriah rubbed his hands together and patted his feet while Gander opened the lid and looked in.

"Nice fish," Gander said. "Who caught him?"

"Burley and Nathan here."

I was glad Beriah included me, but he was about to turn the fish and Uncle Burley and me into some sort of freak show. He'd got to be as proud of the fish as we were and I was sorry we'd let it get out of our hands.

"How'd you catch him, Burley?" Gander asked.

"Caught him last night in the dark," Beriah said. "Ain't that right, Burley?"

Uncle Burley nodded, and Beriah began asking him the same questions he'd asked before, making him tell the story again from the beginning.

He got it all told that time, and after he finished everybody was quiet for a while. Beriah and Uncle Burley had used up all of their talk, and Gander wouldn't help them any. Now and then Beriah slapped his knees and said, "Uhhhhhhh-uh!"

After a while Big Ellis's car pulled up in front of the store and stopped.

Beriah yawned and stretched. "Customers," he said. He went behind the counter and set his elbow on the top of the cash register.

Annie May came in and began ordering groceries. Big Ellis and two other men followed her through the door and walked on back where we were.

"This is J.D.," Big Ellis told us, pointing to one of the men. "He's my brother-in-law. And this other one is William."

J.D. and William stepped up and shook hands with Uncle Burley and Gander and me.

"They work at the same place in Louisville," Big Ellis said. "This is their vacation."

"Well, I'll declare," Uncle Burley said.

Big Ellis sat down on the bench between Uncle Burley and Gander; J.D. and William stood in front of them, shifting their feet and looking around the store.

Finally Big Ellis said, "J.D. hasn't been here for thirty years."

"I grew up around here," J.D. said.

Everybody kept quiet. Uncle Burley was studying J.D.'s face, but I saw that he couldn't recognize him. Gander had turned his blind side to them and was looking at the toe of his shoe.

"Yep, this is where I was raised," J.D. said. He looked at Gander and then at Uncle Burley. "I expect you all remember me."

Uncle Burley got embarrassed then and looked away, and so did Big Ellis. I began to feel sorry for J.D. He stood there waiting for somebody to remember him and be glad to see him now that he'd come back home after thirty years. But he was a stranger to us. I knew Big Ellis had relatives who'd moved away, but he never talked about them.

J.D. looked at Uncle Burley. "You're Burley Coulter, aren't you?"

Uncle Burley nodded.

"And I remember you had a brother."

"That's his boy there."

J.D. turned to me and said, "Is that so? Well, I'll declare. How're your folks, son?"

"Fine," I said.

Uncle Burley looked down at his hands for a minute, and then he said, "Why, I believe I remember you."

J.D. nodded. He looked grateful enough to have paid money for that. I knew Uncle Burley was lying, but I was glad for J.D.'s sake.

"You married Big Ellis's sister," Uncle Burley said.

J.D. nodded again. "That's right."

Uncle Burley laced his fingers around his knees and leaned back. "I was just a boy when you left here."

"That's right, Burley."

After that all Uncle Burley had to do was listen. J.D. talked about his boyhood; and told why he'd left home and how he'd got to be a foreman where he worked and was doing well for an old country boy. He told it all to Uncle Burley, looking at him while he talked. Uncle Burley had said he remembered who J.D. was, and J.D. was Uncle Burley's friend.

"Burley," J.D. said, "it don't seem like more than a few days since I was a boy here, and it's been half a lifetime. I tell you, time goes in a hurry."

"That's right," Uncle Burley said.

Beriah hustled around, waiting on Annie May. He filled a box with groceries and pushed it across the counter, and then we heard him say, "Right there in the cooler, Annie May. Just help yourself."

He looked at us and winked. And we watched her walk to the cooler and open it.

"Ouch!" she said, and slammed the lid down.

Beriah's belly shook with laughter, but he kept his face straight.

"What's the matter, mam?"

Annie May backed out into the middle of the floor. "A stinking cat-fish!" she said.

As soon as they heard her say catfish, Big Ellis and J.D. and William went to the cooler and looked in. Uncle Burley and Gander and I got up and followed them. And then Beriah came, forgetting all about Annie May.

"Who caught that one?" Big Ellis asked.

"Burley and Nathan," Beriah said.

"You might know it would be Burley's," Annie May said. But when she saw that nobody was going to pay any more attention to her she picked up her box of groceries and started to the door. "I'm going home," she said. "If you all don't want to come now, you can walk."

"Well," Big Ellis said. He never looked up when she slammed the door.

"That's a pretty good fish," William said, "for a river fish."

"That's about as good a fish as you'll ever see caught," Beriah said.

William ignored him. "Of course now, you can catch them plenty bigger than that in the ocean." And he began telling us that he'd lived near the ocean once and used to go fishing clear out of sight of land. I figured he was going to tell how he'd caught a bigger fish than we had, and I didn't want to hear it; but he finally noticed that nobody had turned away from the cooler to listen to him. He slowed down then; and Beriah horned in and started telling how Uncle Burley and I had caught our fish.

Beriah stretched the truth in some places and added to it in others. Every time he got beyond the facts he'd say, "Ain't that right, Burley? Ain't I telling them just what you told me?"

Uncle Burley only nodded his head, without looking at anybody. It seemed to me that if he talked much longer Beriah would believe he'd caught the fish himself. William walked around the store, looking at the merchandise, being as uninterested in our story as we'd been in his.

The door opened and shut quietly; when we turned around there was Mushmouth Montgomery wandering up to the counter. Looking as much like Chicken Little as he did, and so lonesome-faced and grieved, it was as if a corpse or a ghost had come in. All of us stood still for a minute, and then Beriah closed the cooler and hurried behind the counter.

"What can I do for you, Mushmouth?"

Uncle Burley went back to the bench, and Big Ellis and Gander and I went with him. Mushmouth's coming made the fish seem unimportant — as out of place there as it would have been at a funeral. We kept quiet, each one dreading the chance that one of the others might mention it.

Mushmouth bought smoking tobacco and a candy bar. We watched him walk toward the door, hoping he'd leave. But he sat down by himself in the front of the store and began to eat the candy. J.D. and William leaned against the cooler, waiting for one of us to say something.

Beriah stayed at the counter, shuffling through a handful of bills. Once in a while he'd thumb one out and look at it, then shake his head and lay it on top of the cash register.

Finally J.D. lost his patience and walked up to Mushmouth. "Say," he said, "you ought to see what a fish Burley's caught. I imagine it's as fine a fish as was ever caught in this river." He said it proudly, as if he and Uncle Burley had been friends all their lives.

Uncle Burley got up and headed for the door. "Well, I reckon we'll get on back."

I went with him, trying not to seem in a hurry, past Mushmouth and out to the road. It was the middle of the morning and the sun had turned warm.

"Boy, we've let it all turn into talk," Uncle Burley said.

Big Ellis called to us; and we stopped and waited while he and J.D. and William caught up with us.

"It's too solemn to stay at the store," Big Ellis said, "as long as Mushmouth's there."

"That Mushmouth's a one-man funeral procession," Uncle Burley said.

We walked to the shack and sat on the porch in the shade.

Big Ellis got Uncle Burley to tell him where we'd caught the fish; and then he wanted to know what size hooks we'd used and what kind of bait. William started in again to tell how he'd fished in the ocean. But Big Ellis had catfish on his mind, and William didn't get any farther than he had before.

Big Ellis said he knew where there was a fish nearly as big as the one we'd caught, and he and J.D. started planning how Uncle Burley could catch that one. William walked over to the edge of the porch and sat down by himself. It looked like he'd never get a chance to tell his story, and I could see that it was beginning to sour on him. He and J.D. had both been strangers when they'd come to the store, but now that J.D. thought Uncle Burley remembered him he'd changed sides. William had been left out. I wished Uncle Burley would pay some attention to him, but he was fed up with all the talk about fish. Big Ellis and J.D. spoke to him and he listened, staring past them at the river.

Jig Pendleton came in sight, rowing his boat down toward the store, and Big Ellis called, "Come up, Jig."

Jig waved and pulled in to the bank. When he came up on the porch he nodded his head to us and sat down.

"We haven't seen much of you, Jig," Uncle Burley said.

"I haven't been getting out much, Burley. But I've noticed you and the boy fishing."

Big Ellis introduced J.D. and William. William only looked at Jig and said hello, but J.D. got up and shook hands.

"I used to live here once," he said. "I expect you remember me."

"Not a single sparrow falls without He knows about it," Jig said. "No sir, I don't remember you. But that don't make any difference."

J.D. looked puzzled, but then he said, "Yes sir," and sat down again.

William stared at Jig for a minute and began laughing.

"What's funny?" Uncle Burley asked him.

William looked at Uncle Burley and then down at the ground. "Nothing," he said.

"You all had any luck fishing?" Jig asked.

"Burley caught one as long as from here to the door," Big Ellis said.

It was about ten feet from where Big Ellis was sitting to the door. Uncle Burley winked at me, but he didn't say anything.

"Burley, if you caught one that big I'm glad you caught it," Jig said.

William got up all of a sudden and started off the porch. "Hell," he said, "I'll show you all how to catch fish."

We watched him go up the path toward the road.

"He's kind of odd," Big Ellis said, "ain't he, J.D.?"

"Kind of odd," J.D. said.

Before long William came back, carrying a paper sack in his hand.

"Where you been?" J.D. asked him.

"To the store," William said.

He put the sack on the porch and took out a half stick of dynamite with a piece of fuse already set in it. He started down the bank, carrying the dynamite by the fuse, holding it away from him as if he were carrying a live wildcat by the tail. Before anybody could say anything to stop him he lit the fuse and flung the dynamite into the river.

After the explosion we sat there, watching the dead fish float up to the surface.

William turned toward us and grinned, without looking at any of us as if he grinned at the empty house. He was already ashamed of what he'd done, but he wasn't going to back down.

"How's that for fish?" he asked.

Big Ellis said, "Burley, do you want some of them fish?"

"No," Uncle Burley said. "Help yourselves."

Big Ellis asked to borrow our boat, and he and J.D. and William rowed out to pick up the fish.

"Jig," Uncle Burley said, "they've got enough fishes to feed a multitude."

Jig shook his head. "It's unblessed, Burley, and no loaves."

"Maybe they'll blow up a bakery," Uncle Burley said.

When they'd gathered the fish and strung them they came up the bank again. Big Ellis went by the porch without stopping; J.D. and William followed him, neither of them looking at us.

"Thanks, Burley," Big Ellis called back.

Uncle Burley raised his hand. "Don't mention it."

After they'd gone Jig said, "That kind of doings is what ruins fishing, Burley."

"It don't help any."

I looked in the sack that William had left on the porch and there was another half stick of dynamite and a fuse. I held it up for Uncle Burley to see.

"Well," he said, "it's good bait."

Jig left then, and Uncle Burley and I went inside and fixed dinner.

In the afternoon we were sitting on the porch again, talking and letting our dinner settle, when we heard a car stop out on the road and the door open and slam. We went around the house to see if somebody else was coming to visit us. Before long we saw a tall, heavy-set man walking down the path through the trees. Uncle Burley touched my arm and whispered that he was the game warden.

"Do you know him?" I asked.

"I know him all right. But he don't know me." Uncle Burley watched the game warden for a minute, and then he said, "He thinks we did that dynamiting."

The game warden came on down the path. "Howdy," he said.

Uncle Burley told him good evening.

The game warden said he was from out of the county, just driving through, and had heard we might have some fish for sale.

"We don't sell fish," Uncle Burley said.

But the game warden wouldn't stop at that. He'd laid his trap for us, and he had to try to catch us in it. "I'm sure this is the right place," he said. "The fellow at the store directed me here. He said you'd been catching a lot of fish."

Uncle Burley frowned when he heard that, and I began to get scared. If the game warden had been to the store there was no telling what Beriah had said to him. And Big Ellis had borrowed our boat to bring in the fish William killed. I was afraid we were half caught already.

"We do all our fishing for fun," Uncle Burley said.

"Well," the game warden said, "if you've got more fish than you can use, I'd like to buy a few pounds."

Uncle Burley looked down at the boat, scratching his cheek. "How many fish do you need?"

"About fifteen pounds."

Uncle Burley thought a minute and said, "Well, we'll have to go get some then."

The game warden turned his head and coughed. "Do you mind if I go along?" he asked.

"Help yourself," Uncle Burley said. He went to the porch and picked up the other half stick of William's dynamite.

The three of us got into the boat and rowed out to the middle of the river.

Uncle Burley looked at the game warden. "About fifteen pounds, you say?"

The game warden said yes, that would be plenty.

Uncle Burley lit the fuse and watched it splutter for a second or two, then he dropped it under the game warden's feet.

The game warden jerked back and stared at Uncle Burley. He couldn't believe it. But Uncle Burley didn't give him any help. He just smiled, as if we had all the time in the world. The game warden snatched the dynamite and threw it down the river. He shut his eyes until the blast went off.

We picked up the fish we'd killed and rowed to the bank.

Uncle Burley said he judged we had at least fifty pounds of fish, and he offered them all to the game warden for ten cents a pound.

The game warden didn't say anything. We strung the fish and he helped us carry them to the road and put them in the trunk of his car.

When we got the fish loaded he took out his billfold and handed Uncle Burley three dollar bills. He said that was all the money he had with him, and he wondered if we'd trust him to pay the rest of it when he came through that way again. Uncle Burley told him that would be fine.

We stood in the road and watched him drive away.

"It's a shame we had to mistreat him," Uncle Burley said.

I knew how he felt. There was no reason for what we'd done, except that we'd all wound up together in the same mess. We'd been having a good time, and now we'd ruined it. "It takes the pleasure out of fishing," I said.

"It sure does." He folded the money and put it in his pocket. "Well, let's go home. We've stayed a day too long already."

"What about the fish fry?" I asked.

"It's called off," he said. "I'm tired of fish."

We put things in order at the house and took the lines up and pulled the boat out of the river. It was getting late. We strung what fish we had left and started home.

When we came to the store we saw that Beriah had hung our fish outside the door so everybody could see it. Flies were swarming over it, and several men were standing there looking and talking.

As we passed one of them called, "Is this your fish, Burley?"

"It's Beriah's fish," Uncle Burley said.

4

There were six of us in the tobacco harvest — Grandpa and Daddy and
Uncle Burley and Gander Loyd and Brother and I — swapping back and
forth from Grandpa's crop to Daddy's to Gander's, taking tobacco from
each as it got ripe from one day to the next; hurrying, because it was a late
season and everybody was anxious and on the lookout for frost or rain.

The weather had changed a little toward fall at the end of the first five
or six days — the mornings cool and brisk and clear, baking-hot in the
middle of the day, and cool again late in the afternoons. Morning was
the best part of the day, when we worked the sleep and stiffness off, and
joked and laughed around the wagons, loading what we'd cut the day
before and left in the patch overnight to wilt, and riding the loaded wagons down the ridges to the barns. The heat built up toward noon, and we
stopped a half hour or so for dinner. Then the long hot afternoon when
we just stood it, driving ourselves to quitting time. After supper was over
we sat and talked around the table until we couldn't put off sleep any
longer, then slept to daylight, when Grandpa called us out of bed. After
the first days, when our tiredness had got to be more than a night's rest
could cure, we dreamed of work, moving through the ripe and golden
rows in our sleep until morning. During the day we'd begun to notice the
little whirlwinds full of dust and dried tobacco leaves that were a sure
sign it was getting close to fall.

We'd worked almost an hour past dinnertime, Daddy pushing us, trying to make up the time we'd lost when he let his team jerk a load off the wagon early in the morning. He stood on the wagon, cursing, mad at himself and at us and at the team, and grieved because what he'd done could have been avoided and because the sun wouldn't stop to let him make up the time, building the load again and calling on us to move faster than we could move. And he pushed us through the rest of the morning, until we quit and ate green beans and potatoes and fried ham and corn bread at the big table in Grandma's kitchen.

Daddy finished eating before any of us and slammed out of the house again, and Grandpa picked up his hat and followed him, hurrying to catch up. Grandpa had been like Daddy once; and now he was old and could only do a boy's work — drive a team or carry water or do the other odds and ends of jobs that saved time for the men who were stronger, cursing the walking cane that he had to depend on a little more every year. He hated to be old and was ashamed of his weakness, because he was work-brittle; what had driven him to work all his life had used up his strength and outlasted it. And even though he was proud of Daddy for taking his place as well as he had, you could tell sometimes that he grieved.

He sat on the edge of the wagon bed while we drove back up the ridge to the tobacco patch, holding his hat in his lap, looking out over the river valley.

We stopped the wagon under a walnut tree at the edge of the patch, and sat down in the shade to sharpen the cutting tools. Uncle Burley used the file and handed it to Gander, then he rolled a smoke and sat looking at the sun beat through the hot air outside the shade.

"You know," he said, "when the first fellow that owned this cut the trees off of it and dragged the logs and brush away and grubbed out the stumps and plowed it and planted a crop on it and an Indian came along and shot him, that son of a bitch was better off."

Gander stopped filing and snickered, his whole face tilting up in the direction of the eye that was out. He filed again, saying over to himself what Uncle Burley had said, and passed the file on to Daddy.

Daddy set the blade against his knee and ran the file across it carefully, stopping to feel the edge with his thumb. "Well," he said, "you work on this damned old dirt and sweat over it and worry about it, and then one day they'll shovel it in your face, and that'll be the end of it."

Grandpa prodded the cane into the ground between his feet, looking out at the sun. "Ah Lord," he said.

Brother used the file and passed it to me, and I used it while the rest of them stood up and began to move out of the shade toward the patch.

Daddy turned around and looked at me. "Come on, Nathan. You'll file the damned thing right down to the handle." He was half joking, wanting the others to hear too, wanting to make it up to us for losing his temper that morning; but still not able to spare any of us.

I laid the file on the wagon and followed them.

Daddy picked up the first stick in his row and stuck it in the ground. "Take a row, boys. Move fast, but be careful." He leaned and cut a stalk and speared it, then another one. "Do your damnedest. That's all a mule can do. I wouldn't ask a man to do more."

He warmed to it, talking himself and us into the work, talking against the dread of heat and sweat and tiredness that always came after dinner and that he felt too. We took a row apiece and followed him toward the other side of the patch.

"Show it to me, boys," he was saying. "Make me know it."

I watched him out the corner of my eye, working himself into the motion of it, his shoulders swaying in the row ahead of us. He worked without waste or strain, bending over his movement.

"Ah boys, when the sweat runs it quits hurting." The sound of his voice had changed — not talking to us anymore, but a kind of singing his own skill and speed and endurance.

I quit watching him and let myself into the work. Sweat stuck my shirt to my back. And a wide swath opened behind us to the edge of the patch.

The afternoon went on, hot and clear, the ground soaking up the heat and throwing it back in our faces. We cut one row and went back and started another. When we ran out of water Grandpa took the jug to the house and filled it. We stopped to drink, and worked again. The rows were long, and the tiredness wore down into our shoulders and backs and legs.

It was lonely to work that way, bending over your own shadow, without energy enough to talk or listen or do anything but push yourself into the row. Uncle Burley and Gander and Brother and I worked along together, not to talk, but for what little comfort it was to hear somebody working next to us, and so we could walk back together to the starting end and joke a little at the water jug.

And Daddy led us. He gained a row, and passed us again, not stopping to drink as often as we did, and not saying much. Only now and then he'd sing out to us, "Follow me, boys — you'll wear diamonds," or, "It won't be as long as it has been."

By five o'clock we could see it was the best day's work we'd done since we started. That made us feel good, and we worked faster, looking forward to quitting time when we could talk about what we'd done and brag on ourselves a little.

Daddy finished a row ahead of the rest of us and came back to where we were. He stood there with his hands on his hips, grinning at us and watching us work.

"Well," he said, "the old man's laying right in there, right there in front all day long. When the sun comes up in the morning and when it goes down at night he's right there, laying 'em in the shade."

It was a challenge, not so much to Gander and Uncle Burley because they had their pace and stuck to it and wouldn't pay any attention to him, but to Brother and me.

He joked sometimes about how one day we'd be able to do more than he could. "One of these days they'll go by the old man," he'd say. "They won't even look at him. They'll say, 'We're coming, old man,' and there won't be a thing for me to do but get over." And he usually wound up, "But, by God, they'll have to have the wind in their shirttails when they do it. I'll tell them that. When they go past me they'll look back and know they've been someplace."

And Brother and I had thought about it and talked about it between ourselves. In a way passing him would be the finest thing we could do, and the thing we could be proudest of. But in another way it would be bad, because it would kill him to have to get out of the way for anybody. We'd told each other that we might never do it, even when we were able, because of that. And both of us knew that if the time ever came it would be a hard thing to do, and a risky one. Once we'd passed him we could never be behind again. We'd have to stay in front, and it was a lonely and a troublesome place.

But once or twice a year, and nearly always during tobacco cutting, he'd have to challenge us. He'd tease us into it. He'd stop and wait for us to get close to him, the way an old fox will sometimes stop to wait on the dogs; then race with us for the love of it, and beat us for the love of it. He had to have somebody pushing him to really feel himself ahead. And always one of us would have to try him. After the race started we forgot what we'd thought about it and went after him for all we were worth; and he'd hold his lead, working as if he had to stay in front forever.

He stood there grinning, waiting to see if one of us would answer him. Then he looked at Brother and said, "Did you notice how that gap between us keeps widening?"

"You'd better go on back to work and be quiet," Uncle Burley told him. "One of these days you'll ask for it and they'll give it to you."

Daddy said, "They've got to move faster than they're moving now if they do it." As he started away he looked back and said, "When the old man's dead and gone I want you all to walk in front of the coffin so you'll know what the country looks like out in front of him."

He went on to the other side of the patch then and got a drink out of the water jug and sat there smoking, watching us.

Brother led us to the end, and when we started back Daddy got up and took the next row. Uncle Burley and Gander and I went to get a drink, and by the time we got to the jug, Brother was already in the row next to Daddy's, starting after him.

Uncle Burley unscrewed the top of the jug and handed it to Gander to drink first, then squatted on his heels watching Daddy and Brother. "There they go," he said.

"It's bad enough to have to work," Gander said, "without trying to kill each other at it."

Daddy glanced over his shoulder and saw that Brother was after him. "Well, look who's coming. If it's not old Tom. Going to put it on the old man today. Look at him come."

It was an old song. We'd been hearing it ever since we'd been big enough to threaten him. Sometimes when we raced with him he'd talk us into a mistake, and then just loaf along in front of us, talking and laughing at us, until finally we'd have to quit. But it didn't seem to be bothering Brother. He was holding his own.

"Brother's staying with him," I said.

"He's getting more apt to beat him every year," Uncle Burley said. "And it'll never stop until he finally does. It was the same way between your daddy and grandpa. For a while there it got to be a race between them just to be breathing."

"Look at the boy coming on," Daddy said. "Look at him lay it on the stick. He don't talk about it, but he's thinking it. Thinking, 'Go ahead and talk, old man. Your day is done. I'm coming after you. Just go ahead and talk while I'm coming on.' Ah, the old man knows. And the old man's going on. The boy may be coming. But the old man's going. Right out in front where he always is. Nobody been to the end of the row ahead of him. And damn few can get there very soon afterwards."

I put the top back on the jug and followed Uncle Burley and Gander into the next rows. We worked along behind them, watching them in the corners of our eyes. They held together, the distance between them strained tight, until sooner or later it would have to break and go one way or the other.

The strain of it suited Daddy. He was happy in it, as if he'd just made the world over to suit himself, feeling the demand on his strength and endurance close to him, and feeling himself good enough. He'd had to work hard for so long, pushed by creditors and seasons and weather, until now it was a habit. That had made him what he was. That was the way he knew himself, and he needed it.

We could hear him, working up the row ahead of us:

> *"He ain't the boss, he's the boss's son,*
> *But he's going to be boss when the boss is done.*

"But I tell you, boys, it's going to be a long time yet. The old man's going through the middle of a lot of days yet with the whole pack behind him. I tell you, boys, when he's dead and gone they'll be standing in line to see what the country looks like without him wheeling and dealing in the middle of it. And it'll be a sight they never saw before."

They finished their rows and went back and started again. Brother couldn't gain any ground, but he wasn't losing any either. That was beginning to bother Daddy, and he quit talking so much. Brother was just coming up to the pace that Daddy had been working in since noon, and that was in his favor. But watching from where we were, it didn't look as if Daddy was even hurrying. He'd made every movement so many times that he could do it almost without thinking about it, as naturally as he walked. It was like watching a machine that could go on at the same speed until it got dark and the lights went out in the houses at bedtime, and on through the night until the lights came on again before sunup. The race had lasted longer than it ever had before, and I began to dread the finish of it.

Uncle Burley straightened up and watched them for a minute, wiping his face with his sleeve. "They're getting serious about it, ain't they? I've seen friendlier dogfights."

"I wish they'd quit," I said.

He laughed. "The last one to drop dead is the winner."

It was getting on toward sundown, and turning cooler. The sun slanted red across the green and gold of the tobacco, filling the spaces between rows with shadows.

Then I heard Brother cursing. He'd made a mislick and it took him three tries to fix it.

"That looks like the end of it," Uncle Burley said. "He's let himself get flustered."

Daddy took up his song again. "Some people just can't work without floundering and falling around at it. But there's always one who can do it all day long and never miss a lick." He kept talking and kept working, and we could see that he was beginning to move away from Brother.

And before long Brother made another mistake.

"Yes sir," Daddy said, "these little boys just barely weaned come out and try the old man. And they want to put it on him so bad, and they work at it so hard. But they just can't quite make it."

Brother threw down his tools and went for Daddy. Daddy turned and met him. We heard them come together, the thump of bone and muscle that sounded as if they'd already half killed each other; and then they went down, gripped together and rolling in the dirt. We could hear Brother cursing, nearly crying, he was so mad and hurt over losing. And Daddy was laughing; from the sound of it I knew that he was in a mood to fight everybody in the world one at a time and would enjoy doing it.

We laid our tools down and started to them. But Grandpa was nearer them than we were. He was in the middle of the patch, counting the rows we'd cut. And he got there first. He waded into the dust they were raising and tried to prod them apart with his cane, but they rolled under him and knocked him down. He sat there with his hat twisted around on the side of his head, cursing and flailing at them with the cane.

We hurried to him and picked him up. Gander brushed some of the dirt off his clothes and led him down the ridge toward the house. By that time Daddy had Brother down on his back and was straddling him, slapping him in the face. He was laughing, his teeth gritted and his face caked with sweat and dust, breathing hard.

Uncle Burley locked his arms around Daddy's shoulders and dragged him away, and I helped Brother up. Daddy stood there with Uncle Burley still holding him, laughing in Brother's face.

"You God-damned baby," he said.

"Go to hell," Brother said. And he turned around and followed Grandpa and Gander down the ridge.

Uncle Burley let go his hold on Daddy, and the three of us walked back across the patch to where we'd left the team and wagon. We didn't say anything. We tried to act as if we'd just quit work and were going home.

When we got to the other side, Uncle Burley picked up the water jug and he and I climbed on the wagon. Daddy started across the hollow to his house.

"Good night," he said.

We said we'd see him in the morning.

Uncle Burley and I didn't talk after that either. It had got quiet all of a sudden, and there was only the jolt and rattle of the wagon and the knowledge of what had happened. Daddy and Brother had fought. It had happened, and it was over. We couldn't think of anything to say.

I felt sorry for both of them. Brother had been beaten and insulted until it would be a long time before he'd know what to think of himself. And I knew that in the night, when he was by himself in his house, Daddy would lie awake thinking about it, and be sorry.

While we drove home the sun went down.

Uncle Burley and I unharnessed the mules and put them in their stalls and did the feeding and milking. It took us until nearly dark. When we finished the work and started to the house, Brother was coming out the yard gate. His face was cut up a little and his lower lip was swollen. He had a bundle of clothes under his arm.

"Boy, are you going?" Uncle Burley asked him.

"I guess I am."

"You're going to let us know about you?"

"I will."

Uncle Burley took some money out of his pocket and put it in Brother's hand. And then we told him good-bye.

A few stars were out. We stood in the gate a long time after Brother was out of sight, dreading to believe that he was gone.

❦

We worked on through the tobacco cutting. Daddy was easier to get along with after Brother left. He joked with us more, trying to make himself pleasant; and even though we were shorthanded he started giving us time to rest before we went back to work in the afternoons. Nobody talked about Brother's leaving when Daddy was around, but we could tell that it was on his mind and that he hated what he'd done. He didn't push us so hard anymore, but he drove himself harder than ever. There were a good many days when he worked in the field by himself until it was too dark to see, after the rest of us had quit and gone home.

Brother's leaving was harder on Grandma and Grandpa than it was on any of the rest of us. They grieved over him most of the time, and it made them seem older. We hadn't heard from him; and every morning Grandma talked about how she expected to get a letter from him that day, and at night when no letter had come she wondered where he was and if he was well and why he hadn't written to us. Sometimes at the supper table she'd remember things he said and did when he was little, and then she'd cry and have to get up and leave.

Grandpa never talked about it when she did. Her grief made him ashamed of his own. And he never mentioned the fight in the tobacco patch, because he was ashamed of that too, and embarrassed that he hadn't been able to stop it. But Brother had been a satisfaction to him, and now and then he'd mention to Uncle Burley or me that Brother promised to have a better head on him than anybody in the family, saying it as if Brother was dead.

After we finished the tobacco harvest we harrowed the ground and sowed it in grain. Then we cut the fall hay crop and put it in the barn. In a day or two after that the first hard frost came. The good brittle days began. The trees turned brown and red and yellow and dropped their leaves, and wild geese flew over the house at night. Uncle Burley and I went out in the early mornings to hunt squirrels in the woods. If Brother had been there it would have been perfect. Uncle Burley and I talked about him a lot, remembering the other years when we'd hunted together.

We spent two weeks mending fences and doing other work that had to be done before the weather got cold. And after that we began the corn harvest. There was no letup in the work, and I was glad of it for Daddy's sake. It kept him from worrying too much about Brother, and as long as he was busy he could take some pleasure in himself. He and Uncle Burley and I worked together, or swapped work with Gander or Big Ellis, watching the season change and planning the winter's work. The cool weather made us feel good, and it was a pleasant time.

Winter set in. The first snow fell and melted, then it turned cold again and the ground froze hard and stayed frozen. We scooped the last of the corn into the crib on a Wednesday, and then slacked off work to rest before we started stripping the tobacco and getting it ready for market. And that Saturday, for the first time in a couple of months, Uncle Burley and I cleaned up after dinner and walked into town. It was clear and bright and beginning to thaw a little. We cut across the fields to the road, taking our time and looking at things. It hadn't been winter long enough for us to be tired of it, and it felt good to be outside with the whole afternoon ahead of us. On the tops of the ridges the wind stung our faces and hummed in our ears, and when we went down into the hollows we could feel the warmth of the sun and it was quiet.

The grass on the hillside was brown, and the trees in the hollows were bare and black except for a few green patches of cedars. Now and then a rabbit jumped up ahead of us, and we'd find his snug nesting place in a clump of grass.

"It'll be Christmas before we know it," Uncle Burley said.

All at once I had the feeling I used to have when I was little, enjoying the newness of the winter and waiting for Christmas. Then I thought about Mother being dead and Brother gone away, and I lost the feeling.

"We'll have to go coon hunting before long," Uncle Burley said. "It's getting about that time."

I knew by the way he said it that the notion excited him. He always started hunting at about that time of year, and hunted almost every favorable night from then until the end of the winter. In the mornings when we went to work he'd talk about what a fool a man was to hunt half the night when he had to work the next day, and he'd swear he'd never go on a weeknight again. But by four o'clock in the afternoon he'd have the fever to hunt; and he'd usually go, by himself if the rest of us were too tired to go with him.

"If this thaw keeps up we'll have good tracking for the dogs," he said.

We walked the rest of the way to the road, planning what night we'd hunt. When we got to the road we saw Jig Pendleton coming up the hill toward us, and we stopped to wait for him.

Uncle Burley called, "Come on, Jig. We'll walk in with you."

Jig came up and said hello to us, and we went on toward town.

"You see that hand, Burley?" Jig said. He held his hand out for Uncle Burley to see.

"I see it, Jig."

"It's putrefied," Jig said. He flapped along with his head tilted up sideways, as sober and dead serious as an undertaker.

"Well, it might be, Jig."

Jig held out his other hand. "There now, Burley, can't you tell the difference? That one ain't. One of them's good and the other one's evil. One of them's blessed and the other one's damned."

"You're in a fix," Uncle Burley said. "You tried a poultice on that bad one?"

"Now Burley, there ain't but one poultice that'll heal her. There ain't but one poultice that'll draw the corruption out of that hand. And that's the poultice of the Holy Spirit."

He'd stopped in the middle of the road and was beating the palm of the putrefied hand with the fist of the sound one. We saw that he was about to start into a sermon, so Uncle Burley said, "Got any nets in the river, Jig?"

Jig hushed and caught up with us. "Aw now, Burley, the water ain't right. The water's got to be right first."

We kept him on fishing for a while, then he asked Uncle Burley how everybody was getting along at our house.

"All fine. We're getting ready to start stripping tobacco the first of the week."

"Tobacco," Jig said. "I used to raise tobacco once. But I quit. I was plowing one morning, and the Lord said, 'Jig, how'd you like for your daughter to smoke?' And I said, 'I wouldn't like it, Lord. It's a sin for a woman to smoke.' And I unhitched the mule right there in the middle of the row, and I left."

"You say you left?"

"Left," Jig said. "I went to fishing then. You know that's where He called them from. From fishing. One of these mornings He'll come and stand on the riverbank and He'll say, 'Jig.' And I'll say, 'Yes, Lord?' And He'll say, 'Follow me, Jig.' And I will arise and follow Him. Aw, He ain't come yet. But He's coming. He's got to get my mansion ready first, but He'll be here."

Then Jig told us about Heaven. He said it was a million miles square and a million miles high, and every street was gold and every house was a mansion. And at night every star was brighter than the sun.

"Do you know why He made the stars?"

Uncle Burley said he didn't know.

"He liked to hear them sing," Jig said.

When we got to town Uncle Burley and I went into the poolroom, and Jig went on up the street to the grocery store. Inside the poolroom it was dark, except for the three green tables in a row down the middle of the floor with lights shining on them. We went past the counter and on to the center of the room, where half a dozen men were standing in a circle around the stove. Big Ellis and Gander Loyd were there, and they made room for us between them.

"Good afternoon, gentlemen," Uncle Burley said. He held his hands over the top of the stove and rubbed them together. "That wind's kind of brittle around the edges, ain't she?"

"We haven't seen you for a while, Burley," Gander said. "Where you been keeping yourself?"

Big Ellis giggled. "We heard you were dead, Burley."

"So did I," Uncle Burley said. "But I knew it was a lie as soon as I heard it."

They laughed, and then drifted into a conversation about who had started stripping tobacco and who hadn't. They talked about what kind of season it promised to be for that work; and from there they went into an argument about the prospects for a good market that year.

After we got warmed up Uncle Burley and Big Ellis and I played two games of straight pool, and Uncle Burley won both of them. The games lasted a long time. All three of us were out of practice, and we were missing easy shots; but after he won the second game Uncle Burley said he guessed he might as well quit since the competition was so poor.

We went back to the stove and talked again. You couldn't remember how the conversation started, or figure out why it should have got to where it was from the last subject you could remember. Now and then somebody buttoned his coat and left. And others came in, letting a cold draft through the door with them, and stood with us at the stove and smoked and talked. The talk shifted from weather to jokes to crops. The wind muffled at the corners of the building. The sound of the fire whipped in the stove like a flag.

Mushmouth Montgomery came in and stood by himself at the counter, eating cheese and crackers; the conversation slowed and hesitated as we turned to look at him and looked away. Since Chicken Little's drowning Mushmouth's face had changed—had turned hollow and blank as if his eyes had given up seeing. And in my memory of him Chicken Little's face had changed the same way; I couldn't remember how he'd looked when he was alive. Mushmouth's face burdened us and quieted us as if we were seeing Chicken Little's ghost. He didn't stay in the poolroom long, and when he left the talk hurried again.

After a while we heard laughter and commotion in the street, and we went out to see what was happening. A crowd of men and boys had gathered at the edge of the sidewalk. They'd caught a stray dog and were tying a roman candle to his tail.

One of them lit the fuse and they turned him loose. The dog ran up the street with the roman candle fizzing behind him, shooting red and yellow and blue balls of fire under his tail. He stopped two or three times before he was out of sight and tried to catch his tail in his teeth, but then another ball of fire would hit him and send him howling off again. Everybody stood there on the sidewalk and laughed. I hated to think of anything being treated that way, and I was sorry I saw it. But every time one of those colored balls of fire flew out and hit the dog under the tail I had to laugh too. The idea of it was funny, and if it hadn't hurt the dog it would have been all right.

As the crowd began to break up and go back into the stores we saw Brother coming across the street.

"Well, I'll swear," Uncle Burley said. "Look who's here."

We shook hands and laughed and clapped each other on the back. Uncle Burley caught Brother in his arms and held him off the ground, hugging him.

I hadn't realized until then how much I'd missed him. I couldn't think of anything glad enough to say.

Uncle Burley put Brother down. "How're you doing, old boy?"

"All right," Brother said.

We went into the poolroom and drank a Coke together while Brother told us about himself. Since he left home he'd been working for a man named Whitlow who owned a farm on the other side of the county. He said that Mr. Whitlow and his wife had treated him kindly, and they had fixed a room in their house for him. Mr. Whitlow had hired him to work by day through the fall and winter and had promised a crop of his own for the next year.

"Well, you've got a good place," Uncle Burley said. "I'm glad to hear it."

When we'd finished our Cokes we sat on a bench behind the stove and talked some more. Uncle Burley and I were relieved to have found Brother and to know he was all right. It felt familiar and good to be there with him, and I hated for the afternoon to pass.

We spoke of Daddy, and Brother didn't seem to be mad at him anymore; but he said that he didn't intend to come back to live with us. He wanted to stay on his own. He was saving his money and planning to buy a farm for himself.

He asked how Grandma and Grandpa were, and we talked about

them for a while. And Uncle Burley and I told him how we were getting along in our work.

Finally Brother said it was time for him to start home. We walked along with him to where Mr. Whitlow's car was parked. The sun was nearly down and there was more chill to the wind.

Uncle Burley turned his collar up and looked at the sky. "It's going to be a coon hunting night," he said.

Mr. Whitlow was standing beside his car when we got there; Brother introduced us and we stood around and talked a while with him. He told us that he thought he was lucky to find as good a hand as Brother, and that we'd be welcome at his house any time we wanted to come and visit. We promised we'd be over before long and we made Brother promise to come to see us.

"Write to your grandma," Uncle Burley said.

They got into the car and drove away, and we were sad to see them go.

On our way home we went around by Daddy's house to tell him our news. Nobody had mentioned Brother to him since their fight, and I felt embarrassed about it now. I dreaded it a little.

It was dark when we came into his yard, and a light was on in the kitchen. We went around the house and called to him from the back door. He answered us and we went in. He was sitting at the table with his supper dishes empty in front of him, eating a piece of corn bread. We pulled out chairs and sat down; and Uncle Burley began telling him about Brother, where he was and what he was doing and what his plans were and what kind of people he was living with. Daddy didn't say anything while Uncle Burley was talking. He sat there looking at his plate and taking a bite off the corn bread now and then.

When Uncle Burley had finished I said, "He's not mad at you anymore."

And then Daddy cried. He didn't say that he was glad Brother wasn't mad at him, or that he was sorry for their fight. He just sat there, looking at his plate and chewing on a bite of corn bread, with tears running down his cheeks.

I could have cried myself. Brother was gone, and he wouldn't be back. And things that had been so before never would be so again. We were the way we were; nothing could make us any different, and we suffered because of it. Things happened to us the way they did because we were our-selves. And if we'd been other people it wouldn't have mattered. If we'd been Mushmouth or Jig Pendleton or that dog with the roman candle tied to his tail, it would have been the same; we'd have had to suffer whatever it was that they suffered because they were themselves. And there was nothing anybody could do but let it happen.

We left Daddy sitting at the table and started home.

"It's bad," Uncle Burley said. "It's bad." After a minute he said, "We're going to have a fair night. Let's you and me hunt a while."

⁂

We hurried through our chores and went to the house. Grandma had supper waiting for us when we came into the kitchen, and Grandpa had already finished eating and turned his chair to the stove. We ate, and Uncle Burley told them we'd seen Brother. They listened while he told them all that Brother had told us.

When he quit talking Grandma said, "And he's not coming home?"

"No," Uncle Burley said.

Grandpa got up then and went into the living room. And Grandma filled the dishpan with water and set it on the stove.

"We thought we'd hunt tonight," Uncle Burley told her.

She nodded, keeping her face turned away from us.

Uncle Burley went upstairs and got his rifle and flashlight and I lit the lantern. We went out the back door and called the dogs. They came, wagging their tails and whining, knowing when they saw the rifle in Uncle Burley's hands that we were going to hunt. There were two of them—Sawbuck and Joe. Uncle Burley let them rear against him. He rubbed their faces and spoke their names.

We walked down the hill toward the woods on the river bluff. Behind us the walls of the house were dark; the lighted windows shone as if they were floating and might twist or slant or change places. On the next ridge a light was still burning in Daddy's house.

When we came to the brow of the hill and saw the house lights scattered through the river bottoms, it wasn't the place of daytime or our memories, but only a distance filled up with night where a few lights burned, the woods and the hunt dividing us from them.

"Well," Uncle Burley said, "they'll grieve in this old land until you'd think they were going to live on it forever, then grieve some more because they know damn well they're not going to live on it forever. And nothing'll stop them but a six-foot hole."

When we went into the woods the dogs trotted off ahead of us, and we walked in the room of light the lantern made, our shadows striding tall against the trunks of the trees. The light was an island, drifting until the dogs would strike a track and give us a direction.

We walked slowly, stopping now and then to listen, moving along the face of the bluff toward the creek valley. After a while Joe bayed a time or two down near the creek. And then the quietness settled around us again and we heard the wind in the tops of the trees. We climbed higher on the bluff so we could hear better, and went on toward the point where the creek valley came into the valley of the river. We crossed the point and climbed down to the edge of the woods on the other side, then squatted on our heels by the lantern and listened to the dogs.

First one of them and then the other crossed the trail and bayed, then lost it, and the quiet came down into the valley again.

Uncle Burley shifted his feet a little, and his hunched shadow swayed against the trees behind him. "They may finally straighten it out."

The dogs worked the trail until it got warm, and then they bayed up the hillside across the valley, running fast and mouthing at every jump, their voices hacking through the dark.

"That sounds more like it," Uncle Burley said.

We started down the hill, taking our time and listening. When we got to the creek bottom the dogs had gone almost out of earshot. We stood still for a few minutes, straining to hear them above the sound of our breath.

"They're treed, aren't they?" I said.

"If they're not they're good liars," Uncle Burley said.

They'd followed a draw out of the bottom all the way to the top of the bluff; and we went up after them, climbing where the streambed stair-stepped down the hill.

We found them treed at a thick-trunked old hickory on the side of the draw. Uncle Burley leaned the rifle against a stump and turned the flashlight up into the branches. We walked around the tree, searching until we saw the coon sitting humpbacked in the fork of a long limb, his eyes glowing in the light.

"There's plenty of limbs all the way up," Uncle Burley said. "You can climb up and shake him out, and we'll let one of the dogs have him."

I set the lantern down and climbed, feeling my way up in the dark while Uncle Burley held the light on the coon. The dogs whined and barked, trotting back and forth under the tree.

I got to the limb where the coon was and eased out on it, holding to the limb above my head. Uncle Burley caught Sawbuck by the collar and moved down the hill. He called Joe into the place where the coon would fall, and I shook the limb.

Joe was on the coon by the time he hit the ground, and they went growling and snarling down the slope toward Uncle Burley. He held the light on them, following them where they rolled and fought in the leaves. The ground was too steep for Joe to get a foothold, and the coon was having a fairly easy time of it. He'd wrapped himself around Joe's head, and Joe couldn't stand up long enough to shake him loose. Sawbuck howled and reared against the collar, trying to get into the fight; and Uncle Burley slid and plunged after him, trying to hold him out of it. The coon kept his hold on Joe's head as if he'd decided to spend the night there; and Joe bucked and rolled and somersaulted through the underbrush, the leaves flying up around them. Sawbuck jerked Uncle Burley off balance, and the two of them scrambled in with Joe and the coon. I saw Uncle Burley's hat fly off, and then the beam of his flashlight began switching around so fast that I couldn't tell what was happening. I could only hear them crashing farther down the hillside, Uncle Burley yelling, and the dogs growling, and the coon hissing and snarling — the beam of light flickering and darting this way and that through the trees like lightning flashes.

Then the light steadied and I saw Uncle Burley dragging Sawbuck out of the fight. Joe caught the coon behind the forelegs and held. That was all of it.

"Whoo," Uncle Burley said.

He picked up the coon and found his hat, then turned the light up into the tree to help me down. The dogs trotted off into the woods again. Uncle Burley slung the coon over his shoulder and I took the rifle and lantern; we climbed to the top of the bluff and started across the ridge.

We were walking parallel to the river again, the valley dark on our left, and three or four miles behind us a few lights were still burning in town. It was easier walking on the ridge, and there were a lot of stars. But the wind was strong up there, and cold. We could hear it moving through the grass and rattling in the woods below us.

At the top of the ridge we went through an old graveyard. When we'd gone halfway across it Uncle Burley stopped and told me to bring the lantern closer. He pointed to a set of false teeth lying on the edge of a groundhog hole that ran down into one of the graves. "God Almighty," he said.

He picked up the teeth and we looked at them. They were covered with dirt and one of the eyeteeth was broken off. "I wonder who these belonged to." He took the flashlight out of his coat and turned it on the headstone, but it was so badly weathered we couldn't read the name. He dropped the teeth back into the hole and kicked some dirt in after them, and we went on toward the woods on the far side of the ridge.

"We're all dying to get there," Uncle Burley said.

After we killed the first coon things were slow for a long time. We went into the woods again and sat down. Once in a while we'd hear the dogs, their voices flaring up as they fumbled at a cold trail, then quiet again while we waited and talked beside the lantern. Finally we got cold and built a fire, and Uncle Burley lay down beside it and slept. He woke up every time one of the dogs mouthed; but when they lost the trail and hushed, he turned his cold side to the fire and went back to sleep. I watched the flames crawl along the sticks until they glowed red and crumbled into the ashes, then piled on more. It was quiet. The country was dark and filled with wind. And in the houses on the ridges behind us and below us in the river bottoms the people were asleep.

About midnight the dogs started a hot track and ran it down the hillside, and treed finally out in the direction of the river. We went to them.

They were treed at a white oak that was too tall and too big around to climb. So I held the flashlight over Uncle Burley's rifle sights and on the coon, and he shot it.

After that he said he was ready to call it a night if I was, and I said I was. We were a long way from home, and since Jig Pendleton's shanty boat was tied up just across the bottom we decided to go and spend the rest of the night with him.

The boat was dark when we got there. We stopped at the top of the bank and quieted the dogs.

Uncle Burley called, "Oh, Jig."

"I'm coming, Lord," Jig said.

We heard him scuffling and clattering around trying to get a lamp lighted.

"It's Burley and Nathan," Uncle Burley said.

The shanty windows lighted up and Jig came out the door in his long underwear and rubber boots, carrying a lamp in his hand.

Uncle Burley laughed. "Jig, if the Lord ever comes and sees you in that outfit, He'll turn around and go back."

"Aw, no He won't, Burley. The Lord looketh on the heart." Jig stood there shivering with the wind blowing through his hair. "You all come on down."

We went down to the boat, the dogs trotting after us across the plank.

"We thought we'd spend the night with you, Jig," Uncle Burley said, "if you don't mind."

"Why, God bless you, Burley, of course you can," Jig said. He asked us if we'd like some hot coffee.

Uncle Burley said we sure would if he didn't mind fixing it. Jig built up the fire in his stove and put the coffee on to boil, and Uncle Burley and I sat down on the side of the boat to skin the coons.

When we finished the skinning, we cut one of the carcasses in two and gave a half of it to each of the dogs. They ate and then curled up beside the door and licked themselves and slept. The coffee was ready by that time. We washed our hands in the river and went inside, ducking under the strings of Jig's machine.

The coffee was black and strong; we sat at the table drinking out of the thick white cups and feeling it warm us. Jig asked how our hunt had been, and Uncle Burley told him about it, Jig nodding his head as he listened and then asking exactly where the dogs had treed. When Uncle Burley named the place he'd nod his head again. "The big white oak. I know that tree. I know the one you're talking about, Burley."

Then Jig mentioned that ducks had been coming in on the slue for the last couple of days. They talked about duck hunting for a while, and Uncle Burley said we'd cross the river early in the morning and try our luck.

Jig gave us a quilt apiece when we'd finished our coffee. We filled the stove with wood and stretched out on the floor beside it. Jig sat at the table reading the Bible for a few minutes, then he blew out the lamp, and we slept.

Uncle Burley woke me the next morning while it was still dark. The lamp was burning on the table again, and Jig was making us another pot of coffee. It seemed darker and quieter outside the windows than it had been when we went to sleep. While we drank the coffee a towboat passed down the river, its engine humming and pounding under the darkness.

Uncle Burley borrowed Jig's shotgun and a pocketful of shells.

"There ought to be plenty of ducks up there," Jig said. "I expect you'll have luck, Burley."

We led the dogs up the bank and tied them to trees, and went over to the slue. The air was cold and brittle, the sky still full of stars. A heavy frost had fallen toward morning; the ground was white with it, and our breath hung white around our heads. When we got away from the trees that grew along the riverbank the wind hit us in the face, making our eyes water. We buttoned our collars and walked fast, hurrying the sleep out of our bones.

We got to the slue and made ourselves as comfortable as we could in a thick patch of willows near the water. Uncle Burley smoked, and we waited, hearing the roosters crow in the barns and henhouses across the bottoms. The sky brightened a little in the east; and we could make out the shape of the slue, the water turning gray as the sky turned, the air above it threaded with mist. While it was still too dark to shoot, four or five ducks came in. Their wings whistled over our heads, and we saw the splashes they made as they hit the water.

The sun came up, the day-color sliding over the tops of the hills; and we heard Gander Loyd calling his milk cows. Then a big flock of mallards circled over our heads and came down.

Uncle Burley raised the gun and waited, and when they flew into range he shot. His shoulder jerked with the kick of the gun, and one of the ducks folded up and fell, spinning down into the shallow water in front of us. Uncle Burley grinned. "That's the way to do it," he said.

He reloaded the gun and we waited again, watching the sky. The rest of the morning the flocks came in, their wings whistling, wheeling in the sunlight down to the water. And the only thing equal to them was their death.

After Uncle Burley and I saw Brother in town at the beginning of the winter, he came home every two or three Sundays to eat dinner and spend the afternoon with us. When we'd finished eating all of us sat around the table and talked a while, then Uncle Burley and Brother and I usually went out to hunt rabbits or wander around together and look at things. We always enjoyed ourselves when Brother was there, and we began to think of him as part of the family again.

When Daddy and Brother were together they were friendly, but they never had much to say to each other. In the months that had gone by since their fight Brother had got to be his own man. He wasn't asking any of us for anything, and that made a difference. While he'd been a boy living with us at home he and Daddy had known how to think about each other. They had known themselves in Daddy's authority. But their fight had ended that; and the old feeling had been too strong and had lasted too many years to allow them ever to know each other in a different way. They were always a little uncomfortable when they tried to talk to each other. Still I could see that both of them were relieved when they were on speaking terms again.

We finished stripping the tobacco crop in the first week of January and shipped the last truckload to the market. And from then until the last of February the cold days came one after another without a thaw. Grandpa said it was the hardest winter he'd ever seen. And for him it was.

It seemed to us that every day of the cold left him older and weaker. He could never get warm enough. While we kept ourselves busy feeding the stock and cutting and hauling wood to burn on the plant beds in the spring, he sat in the house bundled up in a sheepskin coat, throwing coal into the stove and poking the fire with his cane until it roared.

When spring came and the warm days began he didn't get stronger as we'd thought he would. Daddy and Uncle Burley and I put out the crops and plowed them and looked after them through the spring and early summer, but Grandpa didn't go to the field with us as often as he always had. He still got up every morning before daylight, but more and more often when we went to work we'd find him asleep again, sitting in the sun in front of the barn. And he began talking about his death.

One day he told Daddy, "I reckon another twenty years'll see me out." That got to be a kind of byword with us. Daddy or Uncle Burley would repeat it while we were at work, and we'd laugh.

Another day when the four of us were sitting in the door of the barn watching it rain, he pointed toward a corner of the lot and said, "When I die I want you to bury me there."

Uncle Burley laughed and told him, "You've got to go farther away from here than that."

He never mentioned it often, and he tried to keep from showing that he grieved about it. But talking about his own death was a new thing for him, and it saddened us.

It seemed to us that we'd never thought of him before as a man who would die. He never had thought of himself in that way. Until that year, although he'd cursed his weakness and his age, he'd either ignored the idea of his death or had refused to believe in it. He'd only thought of himself as living. But now that he finally admitted that he would die we thought about it too. We couldn't get used to the feeling it gave us to go to work in the mornings without him. He stayed in our minds, and on the days when we left him sleeping at the barn we talked about him more than anything else. We wished he could have enjoyed his sleep now that he was old and nobody expected him to be at work. But he always woke up bewildered and ashamed of himself, and we felt sorry for him.

Uncle Burley was more troubled by the change in Grandpa than any of us. Daddy and Grandpa had argued and fallen out at times, but that had happened because the two of them were alike. They had fought when their minds crossed because they were stubborn and proud, and because they couldn't have respected themselves if they hadn't fought. And Daddy had made himself respectable on Grandpa's terms. But Grandpa and Uncle Burley were as different as he and Daddy were alike. They never had been at peace with each other, and there never had been any chance that they would be. Their lives had run in opposite directions from the day Uncle Burley was born. Grandpa's life had been spent in owning his land and in working on it, the same way Daddy was spending his. But Uncle Burley had refused to own anything. When he was young he worked only because he had to, and Grandpa never had forgiven him for it. They'd been able to live together in the same place mostly by being quiet, and because Grandma and Daddy had stood between them. And although Uncle Burley was a kind man and had as much need to be sorry for Grandpa as Daddy and I, he didn't have a right to. That embarrassed him, and when he wasn't able to joke about it he didn't say anything.

One morning toward the end of July Grandpa rode with us on the wagon to help Gander Loyd put in a field of hay. We'd been held up nearly a week by wet weather; and when it had cleared off two days before, Daddy had helped Gander mow the field. The air was still fresh and clear from the rain, and as we started down to Gander's place we could hear other wagons all around us rattling out to the fields — everybody behind in his work and hurrying.

A heavy dew had fallen, covering the trees and bushes along the sides of the road, and the sun glittered on the wet leaves. The mules were skittish and Daddy leaned back against the lines. They set their heads high and pranced sideways.

"I'll cure you of that nonsense when I get a load behind you," Daddy told them.

Uncle Burley stood up, slack-kneed against the jolt of the wagon, and rolled a cigarette, singing,

> "*Down along the woodland, through the hills and by the shore,*
> *You can hear the rattle, the rumble and the roar . . .*"

After he rolled the cigarette he lit it and sat down again, dangling his feet over the edge of the hay frame.

Grandpa sat beside us, watching the land open in front of the wagon and close behind it, his eyes on it as if it had some movement that only he knew about and could see. The land was what he knew, and it comforted him to look at it. Since he'd been too old to work we'd noticed that he spent more and more of his time watching it, forgetting what was going on around him. Now and then he turned away from it to speak to us of his death, as if hearing himself talk about it could make it real, and turned back to his watching again to be comforted. His hands held the cane across his lap, the skin brown and thin over the knuckles and blue veins.

When we pulled into the hayfield Gander was already there with his team hitched to the rake. "It's too wet," he called to us when we stopped. "We'll have to wait for the dew to dry off."

He and Daddy walked across the field together, picking up wisps of hay and twisting them in their hands to test the moisture. After they came back we sat on the wagon and talked. Once in a while Gander or Daddy got up to see if the hay had dried, but it was past ten o'clock before we could begin work.

Gander drove the rake, putting the hay in windrows. And Daddy and Uncle Burley and I followed him with pitchforks, shocking it. We sweated; the wind blew dust and chaff into our faces and down our necks, and it stuck to the sweat and stung. Now and then we'd see a meadowlark fly up and whistle — a clear cool sound, like water — and drop back into the stubble.

Before long Uncle Burley began to sing. He'd gather a fork load of hay and as he lifted it onto the shock sing, "Ohhhhhhh, 'down along the woodland . . .'" And as he strained at the fork again: "Ohhhhhhh, 'through the hills and by the shore . . .'"

"You must be happy," Daddy said.

"I was thinking about the good old days," Uncle Burley said, "when I was a teamster for Barnum and Bailey's circus. You didn't know about that, did you?"

"Never heard of it before," Daddy said.

Uncle Burley had invented the story about driving a team for Barnum and Bailey to tell to Brother and me when we were little, and all of us had heard it a hundred times. But when the work got hard he'd usually tell it again to make us laugh, and because he enjoyed hearing it himself. He said he'd driven a team of eight black horses with silver harness and red plumes on their bridles. His team had drawn the calliope at the head of all the parades, and it had been a glorious sight. He told about the girl bareback riders on their white horses and the tightrope walkers and the trapeze men and the lion tamers. Finally he got fired, he said, because he whipped one of the elephants singlehanded in a fair fight. He tied the ele-phant's trunk to his tail and ran him around in a circle until he passed out from dizziness. Barnum and Bailey told him that he was the best teamster they'd ever had, but they just couldn't stand for him mistreating their elephants.

Daddy said he supposed it must make Uncle Burley awfully sad at times to have such fine memories of his past.

Uncle Burley shook his head. "I tell you, back in those days when I had three flunkies to polish my black boots and brush my red forked-tail coat, I never would have believed that I'd end up here, sweating on the handle of a pitchfork. It's enough to make a grown man cry."

While we worked Grandpa sat in the shade at the edge of the field, nodding off to sleep, and waking up to carry us a fresh jug of water when we needed one.

"Look at him sleep," Uncle Burley said. "He's living the good life, ain't he? When I get that old I want somebody to wake me up every once in a while just so I can go back to sleep again."

"I reckon so," Daddy said.

"I reckon so. Sleep and fish. That's all I'll do. I'll switch back and forth from maple shade to sycamore shade. And when it's chilly I'll sleep in the sun."

Gander called dinnertime. We fed and watered the teams and went to the house. Gander filled the washpans with water and we washed our hands, then sat at the kitchen table while Mandy Loyd brought the food to us. She was young enough to have been Gander's daughter — slender and well made, and always smiling though she never talked much when we were there. It seemed strange to me that she could have married anybody as old and ugly and one-eyed as Gander. And he must have wondered about it too, because he was jealous of her and he kept her at home most of the time. It made him uncomfortable to have other men in his house; when we ate dinner with him he always clammed up, and nobody ever felt free to joke or laugh. We ate without talking except to ask for the food, feeling as uncomfortable as Gander, and hurrying to finish the meal. Only Grandpa felt free enough to compliment Mandy on her cooking. And she smiled and thanked him.

We went back to work, and Grandpa sat in the shade again, and slept, and woke up to bring us water.

"I wish he'd stay awake," Uncle Burley said. "It makes the shade look too cool and good when I see him sleeping in it."

In the middle of the afternoon when Grandpa was bringing the jug from the well we saw him stagger a little. He steadied himself with the cane and came on; but when he handed the jug to us and Daddy asked him if he was all right he said he'd had a dizzy spell. He looked pale, and it would be a long time before we could quit for the day, so Daddy told me to walk home with him.

He told Grandpa that Uncle Burley had broken the handle out of his pitchfork and he was sending me to get another one. "Do you want to go along with Nathan? You'll feel better when you get home and rest a while."

Grandpa said he'd go with me, and we started up the hill, stopping every couple of hundred yards for him to rest. Once when we stopped he said, "An old man's not worth a damn. He might as well be knocked in the head."

He rested, and we went on again. He climbed the hill almost as fast as a young man, ashamed that I had to wait on him, until the tiredness caught up with him and he had to stop to rest.

When we came up out of the woods, the bottom spread out below us, and I could look back into Gander's hayfield where they were loading one of the wagons. From that distance the three men looked like dolls, but I could tell them apart: Daddy on top of the load, taking the hay as they pitched it to him, placing it and tramping on it; Gander leaning backward against the weight of his loaded fork, his head tilted, favoring the good eye; Uncle Burley making the whole thing into as much of a joke as the heat and strain of the work would allow, the joke ready in the set of his shoulders and in the way he walked from one shock to another as the wagon moved across the field. On the other side of the river the hills were blue, as if the sky came down in front of them.

When we got to Grandpa's spring we stopped to drink.

The water of the spring came from a notch in the rock just under the brow of the hill, and the land sloped steeply around it. The grove of oaks that stood there made the hollow a kind of room where it was always shady and cool in summer, filled with the sound of water running.

Grandpa sat on a ledge of the rock, and I dipped the drinking cup full of water and carried it to him. He drank, then held the cup in his hands, looking at the spring.

"That's a good vein of water," he said. "Nobody ever knew it to go dry."

I thought of the spring running there all the time, while the Indians hunted the country and while our people came and took the land and cleared it; and still running while Grandpa's grandfather and his father got old and died. And running while Grandpa drank its water and waited his turn. When I thought of it that way I knew I was waiting my turn too. But that didn't seem real. It was too far away to think about. And I saw how it would have been unreal to Grandpa for so long, and how it must have grieved him when it had finally come close enough to be known.

Grandpa had owned his land and worked on it and taken his pride from it for so long that we knew him, and he knew himself, in the same way that we knew the spring. His life couldn't be divided from the days he'd spent at work in his fields. Daddy had told us we didn't know what the country would look like without him at work in the middle of it; and that was as true of Grandpa as it was of Daddy. We wouldn't recognize the country when he was dead.

After he rested we started toward the house again. We got to the top of the slope above the spring, and Grandpa stopped, holding the cane off the ground, his mouth open, staring off in the direction of the house.

"What's the matter?" I asked him.

Then he fell. He hit the ground limp, and the wind caught his hat and rolled it down the hill.

I straightened him out and knelt beside him, rubbing his hands and speaking to him. But I couldn't bring him to. The wind whistled through the grass, and the sky was hot and blue, too quiet and lonely to let him die.

I called his name, but he didn't stir. I picked him up in my arms and I carried him home.

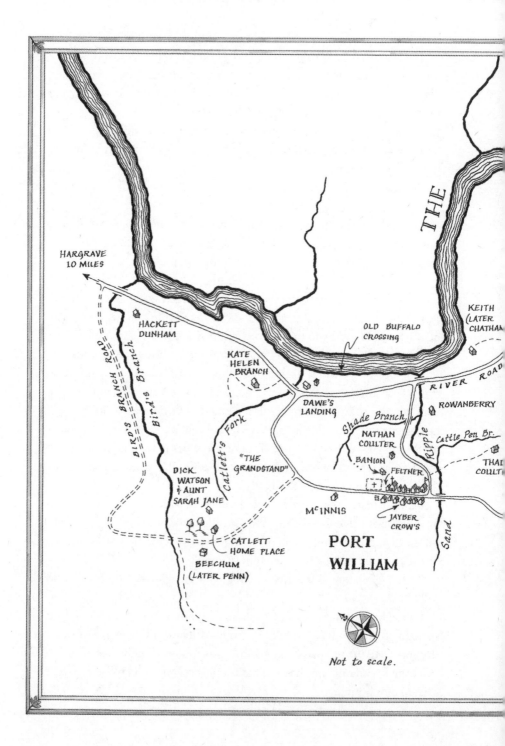

HARGRAVE
10 MILES

THE

HACKETT
DUNHAM

KATE
HELEN
BRANCH

OLD BUFFALO
CROSSING

KEITH
(LATER
CHATHAM

Bird's Branch

BIRD'S BRANCH ROAD

Catlett's Fork

DAWE'S
LANDING

RIVER ROAD

ROWANBERRY

Shade Branch

Cattle Pen Br.

NATHAN
COULTER

Ripple

THAD
COULT

"THE
GRANDSTAND"

BANION

FELTNER

DICK
WATSON
& AUNT
SARAH JANE

McINNIS

JAYBER
CROW'S

PORT
WILLIAM

Sand

CATLETT
HOME PLACE

BEECHUM
(LATER PENN)

Not to scale.

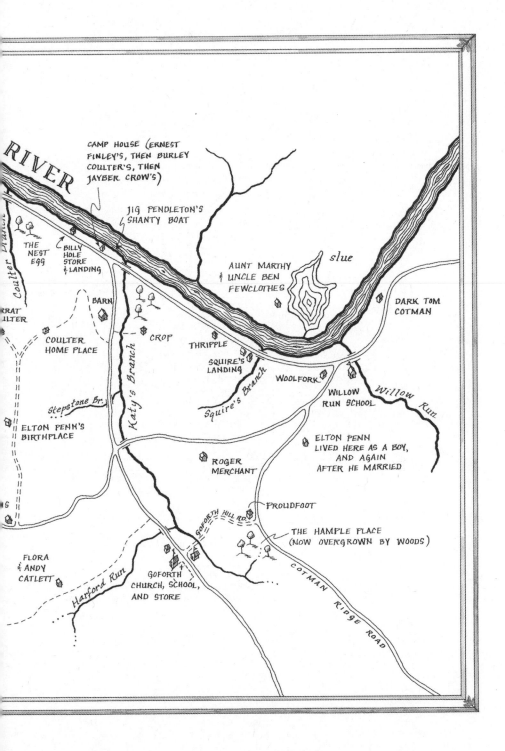

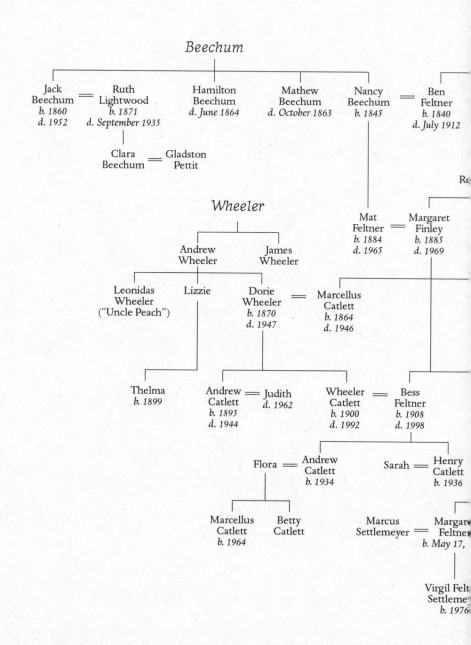

Beechum

Jack
Beechum
b. 1860
d. 1952
===
Ruth
Lightwood
b. 1871
d. September 1935

Hamilton
Beechum
d. June 1864

Mathew
Beechum
d. October 1863

Nancy
Beechum
b. 1845
===
Ben
Feltner
b. 1840
d. July 1912

Clara
Beechum
===
Gladston
Pettit

Re

Wheeler

Andrew
Wheeler

James
Wheeler

Mat
Feltner
b. 1884
d. 1965
===
Margaret
Finley
b. 1885
d. 1969

Leonidas
Wheeler
("Uncle Peach")

Lizzie

Dorie
Wheeler
b. 1870
d. 1947
===
Marcellus
Catlett
b. 1864
d. 1946

Thelma
b. 1899

Andrew
Catlett
b. 1895
d. 1944
===
Judith
d. 1962

Wheeler
Catlett
b. 1900
d. 1992
===
Bess
Feltner
b. 1908
d. 1998

Flora
===
Andrew
Catlett
b. 1934

Sarah
===
Henry
Catlett
b. 1936

Marcellus
Catlett
b. 1964

Betty
Catlett

Marcus
Settlemeyer
===
Margare
Feltne
b. May 17,

Virgil Felt
Settleme
b. 1976

Coulter

Letitia McGown ══ Nathan Coulter

Jonas Thomasson Coulter

...ason ...atlett ══ Elizabeth Coulter — Noah Coulter — Mary Coulter — James Coulter — Parthenia B. *b. 1835 d. 1917* ══ George Washington Coulter *b. 1826 d. 1889*

...eltner *Virginia 58*

Jefferson Feltner

...rnest ...inley *, 1894 , 1945*

Will ...atlett

Thad Coulter *b. 1855 d. 1912*

Whit Humston

Abner Coulter — Martha Elizabeth Coulter *b. 1895*

David Coulter *b. 1860 d. 1938* ══ Zelma Humston

Jarrat Coulter *b. 1891 d. 1967*

Burley Coulter *b. 1895 d. 1977* ══ Kate Helen Branch *d. 1950*

Virgil Feltner *b. 1915 d. 1945* ══ Hannah Steadman *b. 1922* ══ Nathan Coulter *b. 1924 d. 2000* — Tom Coulter *b. 1922 d. 1943*

Lyda *b. 1933* ══ Danny Branch *b. 1932*

Mathew Burley Coulter *b. 1950* — Caleb Coulter *b. 1952*

Will Branch *b. 1955* — Royal Branch — Coulter Branch — Fount Branch — Reuben Branch — Rachel Branch — Rosie Branch

About the Author

WENDELL BERRY, an essayist, novelist, and poet, has been honored with the T. S. Eliot Prize for Poetry, the Aiken Taylor Award for Modern American Poetry, the John Hay Award of the Orion Society, and the Richard C. Holbrooke Distinguished Achievement Award of the Dayton Literary Peace Prize, among others. In 2010, he was awarded the National Humanities Medal by Barack Obama, and in 2016, he was the recipient of the Ivan Sandrof Lifetime Achievement Award from the National Book Critics Circle. He is also a fellow of the American Academy of Arts and Sciences. Berry lives with his wife, Tanya, on their farm in Henry County, Kentucky.